AS LONG AS WE'RE TOGETHER

AS LONG AS WE'RE TOGETHER

BRIANNA PEPPINS

Scholastic Press / New York

Library of Congress Cataloging-in-Publication Data available

ISBN 978-1-338-81407-1

10 9 8 7 6 5 4 3 2 1   23 24 25 26 27

Printed in Italy   183

First edition, April 2023

Book design by Cassy Price

To Carmell, Antoine, and Alyssa —
being your sister means everything to me

CHAPTER 1

So, we're going to Salinger's right after the volley-ball game? I'm just about to hit send in the group chat when I realize my bio teacher has paused midsentence to stare at me.

"All of you. Phones, now," Mrs. Simion says, stalking toward the second row, where my three best friends and I sit. "You can get them back *after* class."

"Has anyone ever told you that auburn's for sure the hair color for you?" I say sweetly. This is the second time today Mrs. S has caught me texting, and I'm not above trying flattery if it means I can keep my phone.

"Novah's right, Mrs. S," Kedijah backs me up, trailing a hand over her maroon hijab. "That shade is giving . . . Met Gala 2015 Rihanna."

Mrs. S is unmoved and takes the phone from my hand. I just have time to catch a glimpse of the text from my big sister:

Ariana: *I need you to cover for me tomorrow night*

1

I scoff at the request, then smile quickly at Mrs. Simion so she knows no disrespect was aimed at her.

"Yes, Novah, my wife tells me every day auburn's my color. And thanks, Kedijah, that's exactly what I was going for." Mrs. Simion collects Kedijah's, Oma's, and Monae's phones too, then takes a step toward Hailee, who was trying, oh so discreetly, to slide her phone into the pocket of her jeans.

"You too, Ms. Triplet. Phone."

Hailee stares at Mrs. S with huge puppy-dog eyes. "Oh, c'mon, Mrs. Simion. This is the third time this week."

"You really want to remind me of that right now?"

"But I promise I was listening." She nods at the mitochondria graphic on the board. "You asked the five functions of the mitochondria, and I can tell you they are calcium homeostasis, programmed cell death, production of ATP, stem cell regulation, and, uh . . ." She trails off, looking stumped.

"Regulation of innate immunity," I chime in, hoping that's correct.

Hailee shoots me a grateful smile before turning back to Mrs. S. "See? We were *both* paying attention!"

Mrs. Simion shakes her head with exaggerated disappointment. "And here I was *so* close to letting you keep your phone. Welp, maybe next time," she says, holding her hand out.

I chuckle at Hailee's pout as she hands over the phone. But I'm rewarded with a smile from her and feel my insides rise. Mrs. S may not have thought that Hailee's sad attempt to keep her phone was funny, but I do. Hailee's only been at Hamer High for three months, and I've never had the confidence to say more than "Hey" outside of convos about class assignments. I find my eyes glued to the smirk on her full lips now, and I want to say something clever, but the sound of our phones landing in the confiscation drawer at the front of the room makes me cringe, and I snap out of the trance.

I turn forward, scooping my sisterlocks into a pony-tail, and mouth "I'll be there" to my friends. I can see the disbelief on their faces—it's been ages since I've had time to hang out after school—but Mrs. Simion clears her throat, and all eyes turn forward.

"Now, class, please pull out your homework on reproduction and cell division and pass it down."

I grab what's supposed to be a finished three-page worksheet and scribble a quick "I'm sorry, please don't fail me. I'll have it completed tomorrow" apology out at the bottom.

I would've finished it last night if I hadn't had to help Korey and Dante with their math homework before going over Bailey's reading-comprehension assignment with her last minute. All Ariana had to do was what she said she would—come home after volley-ball practice to give Miles a bath and put him and Bailey to bed. But she called Mama with some flimsy excuse and wiggled her way out of helping as usual.

"Honey, you got straight As, and you got your Howard acceptance last night. A full volleyball scholarship deserves a break," I heard Mama say into the receiver in the kitchen as I watched, leaning on the doorframe. Ariana will be milking the full-scholarship thing for a while. And it's not that I'm not happy for her too. With a family of nine and a "just making it" dog-grooming business, I know this scholarship was a dream come true for my parents. But why does it feel like I have to pay for all of Ari's failures *and* successes? Why am I the only one ever upset that she constantly bails on us? Especially when Mama and Daddy drilled into us that "family comes first." Somehow that rule applies to everyone but Ari? She gets great grades and a scholarship but fails at helping with the house, the shop, or the kids, and all of that slack falls on me.

But when Mama waved me over with that bright, hesitant smile and apologetic eyes, I already felt myself giving in. She still had bills to pay and lunches to make. And Daddy was still at Lively Pups, on cleaning duty. The least I could do was not be a huge brat about giving Miles, who'd hidden all his string beans in his under-wear, a bath. Even if that meant staying up late to crank out a two-page paper on the three branches of government and complete my bio assignment.

Except I only finished one of those assignments before I woke up at 4:30 a.m., hunched over my desk, to hear Ariana's fresh snores coming from across our room. At least one of us was well rested.

Thirty minutes after Mrs. S confiscates my phone, I'm stuffing my bio books in my locker when I hear "It's detention if you're late to my class again, Wilkinson" from Mr. Lane, my US History teacher, as he zips down the hall with a green coffee mug in hand. I fully roll my eyes, but he's already turned to greet someone else. He breaks into a grin as Ariana bounds down the hall with half of her volleyball team.

"Can't wait to see the team bring that championship trophy to Hamer tomorrow," he exclaims, raising his hand.

Ari reaches up, meeting his high five, and then separates herself from her friends. I give her a side-eye when she leans on the locker beside mine.

"Can I help you?" I ask through my teeth. I have no clue how my sister became Hamer High royalty, but it's annoying. Mr. Lane only hates me as a student because of how much he adored Ariana. It's the same for a lot of our teachers and schoolmates. I simply don't possess the ability to kiss ass like she does. And because of her, I don't have the time to either.

"Why aren't you answering my texts?"

"My phone got confiscated in bio. I just got it back."

She shakes her head. "You got caught on it in class? Do better."

"You were literally texting me in class when Mrs. Simion took it."

That superior look I hate settles on her face as she sings, "Yeah, but I didn't get caught."

I'm about to walk away when I remember what she wants and smirk. She can find someone else to take her shift at Lively's tomorrow. "I'm not covering for you."

Ariana shakes her braids out of her face, giving me an exasperated look. "Novah, you and Zion are so selfish!" she starts. I'm happy to hear our brother refused her request too. Hearing two *no*s in a day must be driving her crazy. I like it. "This is my last senior game. You know how important that is to me."

"And despite what Mama and Daddy and everyone else has made you believe, other people have things that are important to them too. For example, I'll be with my friends after the game because I've covered shifts for you twice this week already and I'm not doing it again."

Ari narrows her eyes at me, but I close my locker with a shrug and walk in the opposite direction. She's at my side before I can blink, probably readying to beg, when I see Hailee walking my way with a textbook clutched to her chest and stop in my tracks.

"I hear everyone's going to Salinger's tomorrow night," she says as she passes. Her voice is light and eager. "Are you coming?"

"Yeah, right after the game," I say, nodding. I stare at her back as she walks away, my chest filling with the butterflies that were just in my stomach a moment ago.

"What was *that*?" Ari asks, looking confused, before shaking her head. "You know what? I don't care. Novah, you have to cover for me! Please? I'll give you—"

I raise a hand, cutting her off midsentence. Usually she'd wear me down . . . or use Mama to guilt me into things, but not this time. I watch Hailee turn a corner and then see Ari pouting. "It's not happening." I'd already intended not to let my friends down, but there is no way in hell I'm letting anything come between me and seeing Hailee tomorrow night at Salinger's.

CHAPTER 2

"Miles, please! Stop with the puddles," I shout as I try to pry Bailey's nails out of my arm. I pull Miles to my side in his yellow rubber duck jacket and rain boots just as he crouches to pounce in a puddle feet away. "It's only a little rain, Bai. I promise the middle school bus will be here with Korey and Dante in a minute."

On an ordinary day, I'd enjoy the walk to our shop from school. First there's the quiet, seven minutes of bliss where I let my imagination run wild and practice lines I'd heard the news anchor deliver the night before. (I always watch the news before bed—there's something about the assuredness in an anchor's voice that warms me and lulls me to sleep.) Then I usually pick Bailey up from her speech therapist, right across the street from Miles's kindergarten. And down the street is Dante and Korey's bus stop at a four-way intersection. By then the peace and quiet's gone, given way to conversations about school, superpowers, unheard-of dinosaurs, flowers, and other random topics. It's a little chaotic but mostly nice.

But today I can't seem to enjoy any of it. It's raining, and I haven't planned exactly how I'm gonna make sure Ari doesn't get her way for once. How do I convince Mama and Daddy to pick my free time over hers? They've never sided with me before, but there's a first time for everything. Maybe I'll volunteer to clean cages, even though the mere thought makes me gag. Or stay late in the shop with Jason and Daddy tonight for closing duty. My phone buzzes in my pocket and I'm tempted to ignore it, thinking it's Ari again, but my eyes slide to my screen against my will.

> **Zion:** Can you cover for me tomorrow night? I wanna take Isabella out to Salinger's

My blood boils, and I feel the urge to launch my phone into the puddle Miles just jumped in, but another buzz lights up the screen.

> **Oma:** It's not a big deal if you can't come. We'll plan something this weekend

I stuff my phone into my jean jacket pocket and blow out a slow, annoyed breath. I'm sick of my friends leaving me out all the time. I told them it wasn't a big deal when I saw the picture of them at Six Flags two weekends ago, but it was.

"You told us you had to cover your brother's shift," Monae had said apologetically. "We didn't want to make you feel like you were missing out."

But it wasn't just the trip to Six Flags. It was the pics of the three of them at Monae's for brunch. And the three of them at the mall. And the three of them at the movie premiere we'd talked about for months.

"Bailey, that hurts." I wince, yanking away from her nails again.

"Thunder and lightning," she signs.

I look down at her big brown eyes against her dark skin and immediately soften. When Bailey was diagnosed with autism as a toddler, we didn't know if she would ever speak, and even now she's a person of few words, but lately she only signs when she's upset or scared. Plus, who could stay mad at a seven-year-old with a baby-doll face like hers? I pull her close to my side, with Miles still stomping away at the puddles at his feet.

The bus screeches to a stop and three kids step off before Korey and Dante tumble out.

"Korey, Korey, Korey," Bailey squeals excitedly, reaching for him as I raise Dante's hood against the rain.

"Look left and right . . ." I say as the bus pulls away.

"And you'll be all right!" my siblings sound off.

"Do it twice . . ."

"And hold a hand tight!"

We step into the street, with Bailey in Korey's arms and Dante barely keeping Miles's wriggling hand in his. The biggest puddle of our entire walk sits waiting on the opposite sidewalk, and just before I can yell, Miles grins back and shoots off like a bullet.

I run behind him as Korey barely misses the tail of his yellow jacket. But before I can grab him, the deafening screech from a car sounds and headlights shine bright on Dante. He stands frozen in the street just as the car stops inches from him.

Enraged, I kick the bumper of the station wagon. "We have the right of way, idiot!" I ignore the frantic man shouting apologies from his window and pull Dante to the sidewalk. "I'm fine," he says over and over as I check for injuries.

"Is there anything I can do?" the man calls, standing halfway out of his car as rain falls down his face.

I crouch so Miles can ride piggyback this time and pretend not to see when Korey flips the man off. The tension's broken when Bailey mimics Korey with just as much gusto.

"C'mon, y'all," I laugh. "We're gonna be late."

◊◊◊

The bell rings as we step into Lively Pups, where doggy toys, snacks, and costumes fill the bright yellow walls of the waiting room. The sound of pups from the back day care rooms seems louder than normal. My dad,

Ezekiel, walks out from behind the crescent-shaped reception desk and crouches his tall frame, gracefully imitating a panther as Miles shoots webs at him. Great, he's in a good mood. Most days, the stress of raising seven kids and running a business barely shows on his face, but then there are other days when I can clearly see the wrinkles bordering his tired eyes, and I know we're all the reason for the sprinkle of gray touching the top of his head and goatee.

Dante and Korey head into the puppy holding room as Antoinette walks out with a broom. "Welcome, welcome, Wilkinson children," she says, over the sounds of dogs barking in the back. Antoinette has worked at the shop for as long as I can remember. Though now she's only part-time since she's in business school and mostly helps Daddy with the books.

Antoinette gathers her long, wavy hair in a ponytail and smiles at me, saying, "Oooh! Someone wants something."

My hopeful eyes narrow at Antoinette, but she just chuckles. Mama always says I'm easy to read, but I hate how every emotion I have plays plain as day across my face. Avoiding Daddy's gaze, I hang my coat on the rack before bending to pick up the jacket Miles left on the floor.

Daddy cocks his head to the side, smiling at me. "Someone wants something like what?"

I ignore the feel of my heart pounding in my chest and tuck a loc behind my ear. Why is this so hard? "I just wanted to ask if it's okay if I—"

"I finished cleaning the cages," Ari loudly announces, cutting me off midsentence. She strips off her gloves, dropping them in the wastebasket before standing directly in front of me, like I don't exist.

When we were younger, people would sometimes mistake us for fraternal twins even though we're two years apart. I used to love the comparison back when it felt like she was my best friend. But now, at sixteen, I resent the fact that seeing her is like looking in a mirror. Yeah, we have the same five-foot-five frame and build, same wide nose and mouth, same carob-brown skin. It's just that one of us is ridiculously selfish.

I roll my eyes, readying to push her out of the way, but Daddy gently moves her to the side. "Hold up, Ari," Daddy says, smiling down at us. "Novah was just about to ask something."

I assume her smug look, resisting the urge to stick out my tongue, but when I open my mouth, I'm interrupted again. The bell rings as the front door bangs open and my big brother comes in wearing his olive-green Acosta's Groceries work shirt under his North Face. Rain drips from the tight coils atop his head onto his face as he pushes his way between Ari and me with the biggest grin.

"Just the man I wanted to see," Zion says, clapping Daddy on the back. "Hey, is it cool if Ari and Novah cover my shift after the game? I have a date with Isabella."

"Absolutely not," Ari says, stomping her foot on the checkered floor. "I'm going out to celebrate with my friends after the *last volleyball game of my high school career*, and you two are covering for me."

"No, I'm not," I shout over her. "And who says you guys are gonna win anyways? There may be nothing to celebrate." I ignore her outraged expression and turn to Daddy with clasped hands. "Can I please go to Salinger's with my friends after the game? I've covered for both of them three times this week already."

"Yeah, because unlike you, I have real commitments," Ari snaps.

"Why don't you try thinking about someone other than yourself for a change?" Zion retorts in my defense.

"Hold up!" Daddy says with raised hands, though his request falls on unwilling ears.

"I already do everything around here!" My arms fly in the air at Ari's audacity, but before I can say more, the sound of Mama's door draws my eyes. She emerges from her office and gives us a pointed look in her long cheetah-print caftan, silencing us all. "I know that can't be the three of you yellin' like that. Didn't y'all just get here?" She kisses Bailey's forehead and raises

Miles on her hip. "What are we arguing about?" she asks, riffling through papers at reception.

"I dunno, Lisa, something about each of them wanting the other two to cover for them tomorrow night so they can do this and that," Daddy says, his stern voice at odds with the calm look that's always on his face.

"Explain," Mama says.

"I need the night off after the game tomorrow so I can go to Salinger's with my friends," Ari rushes, wrapping her braids in a bun. "It's my last game, and Zion and Novah shouldn't mind covering for you both, so you can come too."

Zion's hands fly up. "I— Hold up!"

"Yeah, wait a minute. I need the night off so I can get burgers with my friends tomorrow."

"But I need it off more so I can take Isabella out," Zion claims. "And I never agreed to cover for *anybody*."

Ari whips around at us. "I can't believe you guys are doing this to me!"

"Hey. Hey!" Daddy's voice booms across the room, silencing us. "Tomorrow, after Ari's game, all three of you are to report to the shop."

"But—"

"No buts. I'm sorry, honey. I know we said you might be able to go, and we feel awful about missing your game, but I messed up the schedules and we don't have a babysitter for the younger kids. That's on me, and I'm not gonna make our employees pay for that."

"You're not even gonna *ask* them?" Zion says.

Daddy walks behind the front desk, taking a seat in his desk chair and sliding his reading glasses onto his face. "No, I'm not, Zi."

"But they're your employees," Ari whines. "They have to do what you say."

"No, you're our kids. You have to do what we say," Mama says. "Hey, we made a mistake, and this is the new plan. Now, everyone gets tomorrow morning off as usual for homework and rest, but we expect the three of you at the shop after the game to report for duty."

"And that's final," Daddy says, looking directly at me. "Your mama laid out some food for y'all in the break room. Go have some. All of you. Now."

We all file out of the reception area, but not before Bailey hops into my arms. In the break room, Korey and Dante are already at one of the three round tables, eating from the spread of turkey-and-ham sandwiches.

I slump in my seat between Ari and Zion and make Bailey a plate, but my appetite is gone. In the worst way, I kinda got what I wanted, not having to cover for Ari or Zion for once. On the downside, any chance of finally getting some time to spend with Hailee or my friends is, poof, gone.

"Well, I guess that's that," Zion says, pouring Doritos under the top piece of his bread and taking a huge, crunchy bite.

"I guess." Ari crosses her arms over her chest. "I wish Daddy never opened this stupid dog shop in the first place."

I nod in agreement and my phone buzzes in my pocket.

> **Kedijah:** Nov, are you really gonna meet us after the game, or should we just plan to photoshop you into the picture now lol?

I drop my phone facedown on the table. *Great, just great.* If I don't show up, my friends are *never* going to invite me to anything again. I sigh, ignoring my siblings' chatter, and stare instead at two photos on the crowded white fridge in the corner of the room. The first, the Lively Pups employees huddled together at the Puppy Fundraiser last year. The other, a picture of Korey and Dante with the Johnston boys. And a smile crosses my face as the beginning of a plan presents itself.

"Maybe their word isn't final this time," I say thoughtfully.

Zion perks up. "What? You have a plan?"

"Probably something that'll get us all punished," Ari sighs. "Not interested."

If it wouldn't result in me actually getting punished, I'd reach across the table and smack her. Instead I take a deep breath, choosing my words carefully. I need her cooperation. "Do you wanna go out with your team tomorrow night or not?"

Ari arches a brow. "What do you mean?"

"*I mean* I have a way to get us all what we want. Hey, Korey, Dante, when's the last time you slept over at the Johnstons' for a game of D&D?"

CHAPTER 3

"Why did I say . . . I'd go running with you guys again?" I pant as I hunch over, digging my chipped brown nails into my leggings.

My dad stands in an awkward Warrior I yoga pose on the sidewalk. "There's no air down there, Novah," he laughs, pulling me upright. "And you both came uninvited, slowing me down just to suck up. I still don't know why." Ari and I exchange a quick look. Were we being that obvious? "No one said you had to run with the champ," Daddy continues. He straightens to check his pulse with his watch. "Aye, Ari, you good?"

"Worth it," she huffs, gripping at the stitch in her right side. Even the volleyball star had a hard time keeping up with our dad for the entire three-mile run.

How he wakes up at six every morning to work out while the eight of us are still dreaming is beyond me. I hobble around the corner with them onto Woodmore Lane and see Bailey and Miles playing in the front yard of our corner townhome as my mom bends over her flower bed. The ends of her long graying locs peek from beneath her bright yellow head wrap.

"Lisa, we're done," my dad yells jovially. "My favorite part was leavin' them in the dust. They didn't stand a chance!"

Mama laughs loudly with her head thrown back and every white tooth in her bright smile showing as Mr. Crane grimaces from his front porch. He hates living next to the loudest, biggest family on the street.

"My favorite part was when I beat Ariana," I yell even louder, just to piss him off.

"Oh yeah? Well, whoever makes it to the top step has first dibs on the shower."

Ari jets across the street, spins past Miles shooting pretend webs in the yard, and is jumping on the top step like Rocky before I can find the energy to object.

When I sludge across the street, I only make it to our ugly blue minivan before pausing to catch my breath again. I lean against the too-large mobile Lively Pups advertisement Daddy swears brings in 75 percent of our customers.

"When can we finally trade in this awful minivan for something roomy—like an SUV?"

"When you get SUV money," Mama says, watering her yellow marigolds. "Now, go in and make sure

Korey's not burning my kitchen down tryna make Saturday breakfast."

The smell of turkey sausage greets me as I walk into our crowded living room. There're far more plants than people living here (which is really saying something), several open books Mama put down on whatever page she got bored at, and the tall cubby TV stand our late great-aunt gifted years ago even though Mama hates television. Now it's an altar used to honor our ancestors. Nana Paulette's up there with piercing eyes just like Daddy's, with a dusty, tattered Bible that could always be found on her person. Paum and the flask that was also always on him. Our cousin Lil Jerome, who passed at the age of two, years before I was ever thought of. His favorite pacifier's up there next to his photo. And Aunt Monnie's rose quartz–encrusted locket that holds not a picture but a poem.

I straighten Paum's photo before going into the kitchen to grab dirty bowls and empty them into the overflowing sink. "Anybody ever tell you it's better to clean as you cook, Kor?" I say, smiling as I check the Wilkinson Chore Chart hanging among pictures on the fridge. It's Zion's night to do the dishes.

Korey's eyes keep laser focus as he flips the last tiny pancake and wipes sweat from his forehead. "Working on it."

"Hmm. Well, can I help with something?" I reach for a brown egg sitting in the open carton on the messy counter, but he smacks my hand.

"I told you before—nobody likes crunchy eggs, Novah."

"That was one time!"

"And the last." He returns to whisking some white sauce in a clear bowl, his embroidered apron tightly tied around his waist and bits of flour on his walnut-brown cheeks. "If you really wanna help, go take a shower. You stink."

I roll my eyes at him but walk up the narrow steps, picking up Miles's shoes and Spider-Man toys as I go. I throw them into his and Bailey's room and almost collide with Dante when I turn.

"Mama said you're supposed to be writing a paper, so why does it look like you're stealing my laptop?"

He smiles up at me with a mouthful of green and yellow braces bands and positions the laptop behind his back. "Ari said I could use it to research the *Thanatotheristes degrootorum*."

"Well, you can't. I have homework, and what even is that?"

"His new favorite dinosaur, duh," Zion says from the end of the hall. He hops onto the pull-up bar attached to the door of his and Korey's room and begins his chin-up reps.

"And since when do you care about Dante's favorite dinosaur?"

"Since he paid me five dollars in dimes and quarters to listen to him talk about them."

Dante slips past me and slams his door shut. "Five minutes," he yells as I bang on the door.

"Come eat!" Korey calls from downstairs.

"Give him a break, Nov. He really cares about that stuff," Zion says, hopping down, pushing his black-rimmed glasses up the bridge of his sweaty nose.

I fold my arms and squint at him. "If you know that, then why are you taking a ten-year-old's money?"

"He offered." He shrugs. "Hey, did you hear back from Antoinette yet?"

I shake my head, remembering exactly why I'm annoyed with Ari. She'd promised to help find a baby-sitter, but so far, she's proved totally useless. "How is it my fault Mrs. Waterson isn't responding?" Ari had whisper-yelled to me this morning in our room.

"Because I told you to call her yesterday. You just sent a seventy-three-year-old woman a text at five in the morning when you know she was up late at bingo last night. Of course she's not responding!" I yelled back not so quietly. "I got the employees to agree to work overtime, Mr. Johnston is letting Dante and Korey have a sleepover with his sons, and Zion got the gift card. But you couldn't do this one thing?!"

23

When Daddy poked his head in to ask us why we were up so early, Ari blurted, "So we can go on a run with you," as a cover. She is so bad at this.

Before we left for the run, I shot Antoinette a text. She doesn't necessarily like kids, but we're an exception, and she is our last hope. I still haven't heard back.

Zion strokes his chin, looking worried. "What do we do if she says no?"

My phone chimes before I can respond.

Antoinette: *No problem. Drop them off before the game*

I grin up at Zion before knocking on the bathroom door and yelling, "C'mon, it's time."

Ari swings the door open, already dressed in a purple tank and biker shorts. "Wait, I thought we didn't have a babysitter?"

I'm halfway down the steps with my older siblings on my tail. "We have a babysitter," I say. "Because when I say I'm gonna do something, it actually gets done."

Mama and Daddy are already at the breakfast table eating Korey's pancake sliders with Bailey and Miles.

"A babysitter for what?" Mama asks, exchanging a quizzical look with Daddy.

"And did I hear you say something about authorizing our employees to work overtime?" Daddy asks, resting his chin in his large hand.

"I— Yes, you did. But it's for good reason," I say quickly when Mama narrows her eyes.

Zion swaggers over with a smile so wide we see every tooth as he pulls the gift card out of his sweatpants pocket and slaps it on the table.

I open my mouth to start explaining, but Ariana cuts me off. "We know we pressed you guys with our little 'who's gonna cover who' thing last night, so we thought we'd get a present to make it up to you."

"Yeah," I say, deciding not to call Ari out for pretending she'd actually helped. It wouldn't help our case right now. "We spoke to the staff, and they've agreed to work overtime and close up the shop tonight. Korey and Dante are gonna spend the night with the Johnstons. And Antoinette's agreed to babysit Bailey and Miles until we get back."

"So, this means you guys get to come see my last volleyball game after all!" Ari says, grinning.

"And me and Zion can go to the burger shop after the game," I explain.

"And what's this for?" Daddy asks, pointing a long finger at the gift card. "Bribery?"

"A present," Zion corrects. "After the game, you two can get a bite to eat. And on a *pretty* nice dime, might I add."

Ariana snatches the red card from the table and

waves it alluringly in their faces. As if she did anything to help make this plan work.

"The three of you did this together?" Mama asks.

"More like two and a half of us, but sure," I mutter, dodging Ariana's elbow.

Mama leans forward and grabs the card as Daddy wraps his long arms around her. "Looks like we got ourselves a date tonight," he coos into her ear.

"Curfews," Mama shouts as we head back upstairs to celebrate. "Zion, Novah. Ten on the dot. Ari, eleven. Don't make us regret this!"

CHAPTER 4

"Wait. Wait," Oma guffaws. We're sitting in a red booth at Salinger's in front of half-finished burgers with our phones facedown in the middle of the table. "So, whoever's phone rings first has to do whatever the rest of the table dares them to?"

The restaurant is loud and crowded with a mix of regular diners and people who'd drifted over from the volleyball championship. Ariana and her team are celebrating her winning spike with shakes. Two booths over Zion sits with his arm around Isabella as she kisses his cheek.

"Mm-hmm," Kedijah says. "Your phone rings, buzzes, hoots, flashes, any of that, and you have to do what the table says."

"But nothing that'll get us in trouble, right?" Monae asks.

"Right," I say. "And nothing too embarrassing."

"Embarrassing like finally walking over to Hailee Triplet and buying her a smoothie?" Kedijah asks.

I sneak a quick glance at Hailee, who's sitting across

the room with her cousin, Erin, and their friends. She had asked if I'd be here tonight, but she hasn't looked at me once since I walked in thirty minutes ago. Had I put more meaning to her words than she'd intended? I'd hoped we'd sit together, share fries, and actually talk. But it seems like Hailee had just been making small talk. I take another bite of my turkey burger, nodding. "Yeah, nothing embarrassing like that."

"That might only be embarrassing if she didn't call you 'that cute girl Novah' to Oma in debate class yesterday," Monae says, slapping the table. "I officially deem that as doable."

"I second that," Kedijah says.

"Third it," Oma laughs.

My stomach does a little flip, but I do my best to keep my cool. "Fine, if my phone rings, I will. But Kedijah, if yours rings, you have to—"

My favorite Jhene Aiko song plays, just barely audible over the noise of the diners and a man yelling, "Turn the news up!"

Oma, Monae, and Kedijah explode in giggles. I snatch my phone and of course it's an unknown number. But a bet's a bet, and I've never punked out on a dare before.

When I turn to look at Hailee again, our eyes lock, and this time, she waves. I sigh, feeling like I could melt through my seat. Has she gotten prettier since yesterday? It almost seems like her full cheeks are even higher and her amber skin is glowing against the blue tone of her top.

A woman across the bar is shushing customers for some reason, but the noise barely registers. This is it. This is my moment. I'm gonna go over to Hailee and say hi. I start to stand, but before I can slide out of the booth, I feel Oma touch my hand. I expect her to give me a quick pep talk, but the look on her face steals my breath. Monae looks confused, and Kedijah points to the TV on the opposite wall.

I smile for a moment. My favorite news reporter, Lila Vance, is on the screen in a green rain jacket, but the sudden hush over the diner is so eerie, it feels like my ears have clogged. Until the shot changes to the familiar rainy intersection we take every day.

"Folks, we're following a two-car collision that took place less than an hour ago. You can see here the damage is unfathomable . . ."

A station wagon identical to the one that almost hit Dante yesterday is on the screen banged up and wrapped around a pole.

". . . We're hearing from officials that there were three people involved, and— I'm sorry, can you repeat that . . . ?"

A body bag is shown lifting some poor soul into an ambulance.

". . . And we're reporting two dead at the scene. One in critical condition . . ."

The camera pans to another car flipped in the rain. People around me gasp and some start moving toward the door as a blue minivan becomes clear on the screen. Upside down and just barely visible behind one of the pried-open doors is ELY PUPS in white writing. It's the mobile advertising Daddy was so proud of.

CHAPTER 5

Three months later—August

Bailey and I walk hand in hand, rounding the corner as Lively Pups comes into focus. Just looking at the shop windows from here makes me feel exhausted. Bailey's open-mouthed yawn tells me she feels the same. It's only 2:00 p.m. but I have an endless list of things to do before my head can hit the pillow tonight.

I need to finalize next week's schedule, which is what I was trying to do before my phone chimed, reminding me to pick up Bailey from speech therapy. Ari made the decision to double her sessions, hoping to prove to the judge that she was serious about getting us all back on track. But Bailey still hasn't spoken a word to any of us other than Miles since the night of the accident. In my opinion, it's a waste of time. She still signs, and communication is communication. We all know ASL, Mama made sure of it. Plus, now she always carries the little dry-erase board that

Zion bought for her a week after the accident so she can speak to everyone. But it wasn't my choice, and more often than not, Ari prefers I don't chime in with my opinions anyways.

After I finalize the schedule, I need to send bill-reminder emails to all our customers who are more than three days behind on payments; get a handle on my summer reading, math, and history packets before school starts next week; and then it's my night to do the laundry. We only reinstated our Wilkinson Chore Chart last month after our first surprise visit from Ms. Lusby, our assigned social services rep. The house wasn't dirty, but there were more dishes in the sink and dirty clothes pouring out of the laundry room than any of us would've liked for Ms. Lusby to see. Her disapproving glances sent my heart fluttering at triple speed, but she only suggested Ari come up with a way to structure the housework so that we could all contribute equally. Ari rushed to find the chore chart under a stack of mail on the kitchen counter and promptly set it back on the fridge before Ms. Lusby left.

The red HELP WANTED sign in the window draws a heavy sigh out of me when I look up. Zion was supposed to be scheduling interviews with our current applicants, but he's been so distracted lately. We need to hire someone before all of us go back to school, leaving only Ari and the employees who actually show up. Honestly, I wish I could just stay at the shop and avoid school altogether. I boop Bailey's nose, making a mental note to add "interviews" to my list as she holds the door open for me.

◊◊◊

I finally slap my pen down after an hour of planning the perfect, accommodating employee schedule for the upcoming week. I didn't used to give my parents enough credit for how hard it was to do these little tasks like scheduling to keep the shop running. I hadn't realized how little my siblings and I actually did to keep a steady income flowing, employees content, or a happy, healthy family. Currently, Ari, Zion, and I aren't exactly leveling up, but they'd made this look a whole lot easier than it is. I look up to see the four-month-old Post-it note stuck to the computer screen in Daddy's handwriting:

A day's only as good as you make it ☺

I smile at the note, fighting back tears. Daddy was always so great at being the cheerleader in our family. But now the note only reminds me of how tough it is to have good days with them gone, despite how hard I try. When I feel my bottom lip tremble, I suck in a breath, stopping myself from tumbling down that rabbit hole, and push back from the reception desk, spinning in the chair.

"Antoinette, it's done!" I call, and she looks up from the box of dog collars she was restocking.

"Jason has to take his daughter to gymnastics at two twice a week? That's okay, 'cause I got Zion pulling up the grooming slack. Antoinette, you need the weekends off for your new class? It's all good. School's out, and Violet can cover those shifts. Ari has to leave early on Thursday for an interview? Oh, I solved that problem yesterday. Carlie's coming in early to handle day care room two."

"We did it!" Miles jumps to reach my high five and lands in a superhero crouch.

Antoinette bends to look at the schedule, then glances at me and back at the schedule again. "You didn't talk to Ari?" she asks with a grimace.

I glance at my watch and shake my head. "She's supposed to be here right now to cover reception so I can take over room two for Junie. Oh, and have you spoken to Violet? I haven't been able to get ahold of her all day."

Mrs. Lucas, an older red-haired regular, walks in then, followed by a man with a ponytail who asks for a boarding pamphlet before taking a seat. "I'll buzz for Riggles, Mrs. Lucas. He'll be out in three minutes!"

Antoinette lowers her voice. "Okay, honey. You may want to sit for this."

"I am sitting."

"Right . . . so, Violet quit today."

Instinctively, I jump out of my seat. "What! When?"

"Sometime this morning before Ariana fired Carlie."

Furious, I grab my phone to call Ari, but the reception phone rings.

"My shift's done, but I'll see you tomorrow," Antoinette says, grabbing her purse from beneath the desk. "Hear Ari out when she gets here, okay? Everybody's doing their best, and if we hadn't lost Carlie and Violet today, your schedule would've been perfect!"

I wave her out and bring the receiver to my ear when the bell rings again and a tall man carrying a squiggling bulldog puppy with a wet snout and tan fur enters. He follows the dog's excited barks and immediately heads for the toy wall. "Hello, this is Novah speaking at Lively Pups, where we make all your pup's day care, grooming, and boarding dreams come true."

Bailey bounds out carrying Riggles, the black-and-white schnauzer, and hands him to Mrs. Lucas. The look on her face tells me she has an issue, but I hold up a finger, mouthing, "One moment," before she can approach reception.

"Yes, we can . . . Please hold. Hi, Mrs. Lucas, is there a problem?"

"Well, yes. Obviously," she rasps, holding the dewy-eyed schnauzer up as if whatever problem there is, is apparent. "His cut. It's a mess!" She pokes at the style chart taped to the counter. "I asked for number ten, a mild trim, but to leave her tail long." I look from Riggles to the cut Mrs. Lucas is jabbing at and grimace at Zion's groom-work. What was supposed to be a mild cut has left Riggles nearly bald with a beard, for some reason, and looking more like an overgrown rat than a schnauzer. "Now she'll get cold!" Mrs. Lucas whines.

"It's August," Dante exhales, exiting the back room, followed by Jason, our bushy-haired canine coach.

"Did one of you do this to my Riggles?" Mrs. Lucas asks, thrusting a finger at them.

I shift to stand in front of Dante. "A morning-shift employee groomed Riggles. Jason, do you mind helping our other customers?"

"You know, *I'm* a pretty loyal customer, and Ezekiel always gets his cuts right!"

The sound of Daddy's name makes my stomach flip, bringing on a sudden wave of nausea, but before any dread can move in, the phone rings again. I clear my throat, trying to cover up what I hope wasn't a visible reaction, and pick up the receiver. "Uh, just one second, ma'am. Hello, this is Novah speaking at Lively Pups. Please hold."

"No, I won't wait another second. Riggles looks like a rat!" she shouts, confirming my comparison. It might be funny if she wasn't turning red in the face. "Ezekiel promised that he would personally care for all of Riggles's grooming needs—"

"I—"

"And kept that promise for over a year, so that's who I'd like to speak to!" Her voice ticks up in volume, turning eyes from every corner of the room, and I wish to myself that Antoinette hadn't left when she did. She's so much better at handling irate customers than me.

Bailey pulls on my sleeve, signing, "I need a snack."

"Just a moment, Mrs. Lucas. Yeah, Bails, that's a good idea. Dante, I packed a lunch box and it's in the fridge in the break room. Take Miles too, please."

As they round the corner, the doorbell rings again, and Zion and Ari enter. I nod them over to handle Mrs. Lucas, raising a finger, once again for her patience. But as I go to pick up the phone, she slaps her hands on the counter, making Riggles jump in her arms.

"I can't understand why he would leave you in charge. Now, I said! I want to speak to Ezekiel now. He'd never let this happen to—"

"Ezekiel is dead," I say in a raised voice, struggling

to keep my tone even. "My dad is dead, okay? I'm sorry, but you cannot demand to speak to dead people about your dog-grooming concerns."

Mrs. Lucas's outrage turns to shock as she stares wide-eyed, at a loss for words.

I allow my professional smile to settle on my face, swallowing the urge to curse out a customer as everyone in the room, including the dogs, stares at me open-mouthed and wide-eyed.

"If you'd just given me a moment like I asked, you may have found it in you to look around, and you would've seen my parents' obituaries on the noticeboard. But now you have my full attention, and we *so* appreciate your business, so if you just give me a moment to finish up this call, we can discuss your needs."

"Actually," Ari says, rushing forward with a fake smile plastered on her face, "I'm gonna take over and, um—" Her eyes dash around the room in a panic until they land on the stack of coupons lying in front of my forgotten algebra summer packet. She grabs the stack, saying, "Maybe we can discuss what went wrong and figure out how exactly we can be sure to keep your business?"

I want to gag at the obvious desperation in her voice, but it turns out to be exactly what Mrs. Lucas wanted to hear because she says, "That sounds more like it," with her snooty nose in the air.

"Zion, can you handle the calls? Novah's gonna take a little break, and I'll be back there in five so we can talk."

I keep my own fake smile and say, "There are customers waiting on lines two and three," through gritted teeth as I turn sharply.

"Whoo, the *attitude* on that girl," I hear Mrs. Lucas sigh as the door closes behind me.

◊◊◊

Thirty minutes later, I'm sitting in the break room with Bailey, Miles, and Dante when I hear Ari's angry stomps from outside the door. "Novah, what the hell was that?" she fumes. "Where do you get off speaking to well-paying customers like that?"

"Relax, Ari," Zion says, following behind her. "I'm seventy-five percent sure Novah wouldn't have gone off if the woman didn't deserve it!"

I'm taken all the way back. "What? I didn't go off on her! Even though, yeah, she deserved it. Plus, you saw how she was. We don't *need* her business."

"I'm sorry," Ari says, coming up to my chair with folded arms. "Maybe you need to sit down with me and Antoinette next time we go over the books so you can see just how much we need everyone's business."

39

"Mama never would've let somebody speak to me like that," I retort.

"Mama's not here. I am!"

"Y'all, let's just . . . all take a breather," Zion sighs, standing between us.

But I sit back in my chair, viewing Ari through narrowed eyes. "If you'd been here to cover reception like you said you would, it wouldn't have happened," I say, somehow managing to keep my tone level. "Having the title of a legal guardian doesn't put you in charge of everything. You think you can just dish out the money, fire whoever you want, and make all the decisions. We're supposed to be doing this together."

Ari looks at me, bewildered, as if I'm missing something obvious. "We may be doing this together, but at the end of the day, what I say goes. I'm the reason we're all still together!"

"Yeah, and that's what you were supposed to do, Ari!"

"Supposed to?" she scoffs. "No, I'm supposed to be prepping to go to Howard in the fall on a volleyball scholarship. I'm sacrificing all of that for y'all."

After Mama and Daddy died, Ari not only had to turn down her volleyball scholarship but also her acceptance to Howard completely. She couldn't go to DC for school anymore. Not when there was a shop to run and bills to be paid. Especially not when the state tried to split us up.

Despite all the drama between us, my heart broke for Ari when she made the call to admissions. All those late nights studying and her hard work practicing had been for nothing. But Ari's not the only one making sacrifices to keep our family afloat.

I shake my head in disbelief. "What do you want? A pat on the back? We've thanked you a million times. What else do you want? A medal?"

"I don't need a *medal*," she says through her teeth, coming down on me. "I need you to listen, and do what I say when and however I ask you to do it. The judge granted custody to *me*!"

"Conditionally," I say quietly. Though that's not just a jab thrown at Ari. It's a threat to all of us. Because she's so young and there's so many of us, Ari was only granted conditional custody back in May. She has until January to prove to Judge Odell that she is a capable guardian. That means running the shop to maintain a steady income, keeping a roof over our heads and all of us out of trouble. She also has to ensure that everyone keeps their grades up, appointments are kept, individual goals are met, and most importantly, we need to pass inspection at all of our scheduled *and* surprise home visits with our caseworker. There are only five months until our deadline, and things are shaky at best.

I know I struck a nerve before Ari even opens her mouth.

"I'm sorry," Ari says sweetly, her voice dripping with fake concern. "Would you rather us all be separated because of one of your stupid blowups? You want Ms. Lusby to find a nice two-parent foster home for you to live in instead?"

"Ari," Zion says. His tone is a warning, but she doesn't stop, and suddenly my eyes are locked on hers.

"Maybe you can find some other ungrateful sixteen-year-olds with bad attitudes and smart-ass mouths to buddy up with in a group home?"

I purse my lips, finally looking away from Ari so she can't see the tears prickling my eyes.

"That was mean, Ari," Dante says quietly, reminding us that we aren't alone.

Miles and Bailey are still here too, and I look at each of their concerned and confused eyes and slap a weak smile on my face.

"No, it's fine, Dante," I say, grabbing my book bag up from the floor. "I'm gonna go home to redo the employee schedule and get started on the laundry, and I'll see you guys when you get there, okay?"

"No, Novah, wait," Zion says, motioning for Ari to say something.

I look at her expectantly, and for a moment, it looks like she's considering something—I don't know what. But then her eyes harden and a stony resolve settles on her face. "Send out the schedules to everyone before eight," she says before whisking out of the room.

I shove my rickety chair under the table, avoiding my siblings' eyes before rushing out too.

◊◊◊

I've grown used to seeing Nana Paulette, Paum, Lil Jerome, and Aunt Monnie in their spots on our TV stand altar for years now. But I haven't quite gotten used to the heartbreak of seeing Mama and Daddy up there. At first, I was enraged every time I passed by and refused to look their way, but seeing Korey meditate, reflect, and pray here with such devotion made me grateful that he'd found a way to let peace back in, even if I haven't yet.

I light the white candle sitting beside their photo and bend at the knees, craning to see them at the top. It's silly, but sometimes I swear Mama's smile is so bright I need to take a deep breath before I even attempt to take it all in. And Daddy's laugh, I can hear it—crystal clear now. When I even glance that way, I feel his deep baritone chuckle surrounding me. Holding me. A silver chain Bailey found while digging around in their room holds the wedding rings now draped over their photo.

Mama always said the ancestor altar wasn't about worship, like at church—but connection. Reconnecting where we were cut off in this life . . . in this realm.

Picking up where we left off. Or even where we feel abandoned. It's a source of strength and an avenue to gain knowledge, as long as we're willing to let them guide the way. I never really paid too much attention to this altar. Though I'd often see Mama kneeling in front of it like I am now. But no matter how painful it is to see them up there and how odd it is to view them as ancestors, that's the title they now hold.

"What would you want beside your picture?" Korey asks, startling me from behind the couch.

"I dunno," I whisper. "There's nothing that's really always on me. And nothing I own feels like it defines even a part of who I am. It doesn't matter anyways, does it? The people you leave behind decide what goes with you on the altar."

Korey takes his place on bended knee, beside me. "Well, I'm telling you now, don't let anybody put anything up there next to me but my apron."

I nod. "You think they'd be proud of us, Kor? How we're gettin' on?"

He snorts. "We fight all the time. The dishwasher's been broken for three weeks. Somebody forgot to go grocery shopping. I gotta pass summer school if I wanna make it to the eighth grade. And we're kind of a mess. They'd give us a solid five outta ten. Wouldn't even have to ask."

"Yeah, I guess we've all been half-assing life

since . . ." I clear my throat. "What do you think about how Ari's handling us? Considering."

"Considering who she was before and who we are now?" He shrugs. "She's trying. I'll give her props for that."

I remember the overwhelming sensation of relief when Judge Odell granted Ari custody, even if it was conditional. We could stay in our home, together. That's all that mattered.

But it could all fall apart at any moment. If Ms. Lusby caught us on a bad day, it'd be all over. If Ari lost custody, our family would be torn apart. They say they try to keep siblings together, but I'd bet a good amount of money that there aren't many foster parents clawing to welcome six siblings ranging from five to seventeen into their homes. No, no matter what, we have to make sure Ari is granted permanent custody at the hearing next January. There are days when I'd much rather play in traffic than speak to Ari, but if listening and being cordial for the next five months is what it takes for her to be granted full custody, I can probably do that. The alternative is unimaginable. I can't allow it to happen.

CHAPTER 6

I hadn't been in school for more than five minutes on my first day of junior year before some senior tapped my shoulder in the busy hall.

"Wilkinson, right?"

I looked up at the tall kid with an eyebrow piercing, eyes full of woe, and gave a regretful nod.

"I was in Salinger's the night the news announced the accident and saw how everything went down. My dad's a pastor and I put your name in the prayer box, so our congregation's been praying for you this entire summer."

At mention of the accident, my heart seemed to skip a beat, but I forced a smile on my face. "That's really kind. Thanks," I said. And I'd meant it, but I wished he'd just let me walk away then.

Instead, he said, "If there's anything I can do for you, please let me know."

It was that phrase that irritated me most. Too often it came from near strangers, from acquaintances, and from people who didn't actually mean the "anything" part. Hell, Isabella had said it to Zion and just broke up with him six days ago. Most people struggle with what to say to a person who's grieving. And I get it, it's awkward. Because in all honesty there's rarely ever a *right* thing to say. No amount of condolences, thoughts, prayers, or good vibes sent our way could make the situation better. But at the same time, so many people feel like they can't say nothing. So *"If there's anything I can do, please let me know"* becomes standard.

But I knew that, like most people who'd ever said it, he didn't mean any harm, so I said, "I appreciate that," with my signature closed-mouth smile and kept it pushin'.

I wish that was my only incident at school, but three more came before lunch. There was Fiona, last year's freshman class president, who silently slid over a Hallmark sympathy card, signed by several classmates. Some kid from Spanish II never actually mentioned my parents but kept a running commentary about loss in terms of his turtle who passed away last week. And worst of all Ms. Brooks, in homeroom, tried to make the vague announcement that "we never know what people are going through, so we should be kind at all times," while simultaneously staring me dead in the eyes from the front of the classroom.

Now I sit in the raucous cafeteria with Kedijah,

Oma, and Monae while Principal Jay talks about some science fair over the loudspeaker. Because of all our busy summer jobs, this is the first time all four of us have been together since the funeral. And it feels . . . almost normal.

"Wanna try some?" Kedijah asks, bringing me back to the conversation. Oma's camera swings to me as Kedijah holds up what looks like a flattened see-through piece of jerky in my face.

"Guess what it is," Monae says, barely holding back a laugh.

I squint sideways at it with a frown. "I'm not sure, but I wanna say it's definitely not food."

Oma and Monae guffaw.

"No, smart-ass." Kedijah smirks. "It's rice paper bacon. I made it last night at our annual back-to-school sleepover."

I kind of remember Oma mentioning that to me last week on FaceTime, but I'd completely forgotten. It doesn't bother me as much that I missed it this year. I was too busy helping Korey pack lunches, ironing clothes with Dante, and scrambling to get my math packet done to even think about the sleepover. But a tiny piece of me knows that if I had, I would've been there to see Kedijah's rice paper bacon disaster in action. Or even had the slightest idea what Monae and Oma were talking about when they kept saying "around the bark and up the tree" randomly throughout the day. I'd gathered it was from some Netflix show they all binged together. At this point, I'm just lucky they still consider me a friend after I'd all but neglected them this summer when they were there for me. I was lucky they were the type of people who meant the words *If you need anything, let us know."* None of my calls or texts ever went unanswered. They were emergency babysitters, a shoulder to cry on, and listening ears when I needed to vent. Even if they didn't understand what I was dealing with, they were trying their best and deserved a more reliable friend.

Feeling suddenly guilt-ridden, I lean forward and grab a piece of bacon, pop it in my mouth, and force a smile as I chew with Kedijah's hopeful eyes on me. "It . . . tastes bacon-ish."

"Yeah," Oma says. "Almost like it was bacon in a past life, but didn't quite make the cut this time around."

I belly laugh, grabbing a napkin to spit the fake bacon into.

The conversation drifts into trash-talking Mr. Lane, our World History teacher this year, and how he gave me the "excuses are bridges to nowhere . . ." speech in front of the whole class when he discovered I hadn't done his summer reading.

When Oma calls him a self-centered jackass, I chuckle, and mayo from my turkey burger misses my mouth and falls on my nude-brown tank.

I stand to toss the napkin I used to clean myself up into a nearby can and catch Hailee's eye a few tables away. Blood immediately rushes to my face. When she flashes a hesitant smile, I'm only able to give an awkward wave before doing an even more awkward about-face and slumping back to my seat.

"Novah, that was hard to watch," Kedijah says as I palm my forehead.

"I know, I know . . ."

"Why didn't you say something?" Monae asks.

I blush and look away. "Because I ran into her last week when I was grocery shopping with Zion, and when I saw her . . . I just couldn't face her. But she definitely saw me going out of my way to avoid her."

Oma's eyes are full of concern. "And why couldn't you face her?"

I bite my lip for a moment. I know it's silly, but I'm embarrassed by how Hailee saw me react after seeing the crash on the news at Salinger's. I know I'm probably overthinking things—like, who's gonna judge me for breaking down in hysterics on the worst day of my life? But it just makes me uncomfortable, knowing that she witnessed it. Before I can even try to explain,

I'm saved by a freckle-faced girl who seems to have just materialized beside me.

"Hey, Novah. Can I talk to you for a sec?" she asks. Her maroon curls peek out of her head wrap as she waits with a kind expression.

I nod before following her toward the recycling receptacles a few feet away.

"I'm not sure if you know me or not. I'm Summer."

I nod. "You're a junior, right? We were both in the Pride group last year." I don't mean to sound curt, but I know what she's gearing up to say, and I'd rather us just get it over with.

"Yep. That's me." Her eyes are filled with a ridiculous amount of compassion. "I just want to offer my condolences to you and your family and let you know that even though we never talked much, I'm here for you."

I nod a closed-mouth thank-you and turn to leave, but she continues, "Our mothers were pretty friendly."

That makes me pause. I turn back to her.

"Our dads too."

Now that my parents are gone and I can't create new memories with them, the idea that someone might have something new to share about them makes my heart jump. "What's your last name again?"

"Becker," she says.

"Right. Your parents own that apothecary in Clinton."

"Mm-hmm. I didn't want to bother you last year when it was still so fresh. And I'm sure it still is. But your mom frequented our store, and when I tell you her smile literally lit up dark spaces, I mean it. And your dad was the only one who could get my schnauzer, Rugby, calm enough for a good cut. They were both so—"

A familiar burning stings the back of my eyes, and before I can stop it, I'm swiping at tears with the back of my hand. "I'm sorry. I don't mean to cut you off, but I already know all that about my parents." I wrap my arms around myself and rock back on my heels.

"Right—right. I apologize," she says, reaching out to touch my arm, but I flinch and pull away, suddenly feeling like my own arms hugging myself are the thin thread holding me together. "Sorry, again. Uh, my point is that I head the Student Grief Support Group here, and I thought I'd personally invite you to a meeting."

What was one tear has turned to a silent stream. That's how it always is. That's why I keep my walls so high. Seeing me fall apart or burst into tears doesn't help my baby brothers and sister heal, so I don't. Sulking won't bring customers in the door at the shop.

Summer hands me a paper from her satchel with the SGSG's meeting info, and I crumple it in my hands with my eyes shut tight . . . I can feel it coming on. "You're the one who was putting these in my locker every day during the last week of school?"

She nods. "It's just that . . . five years back, I lost my baby brother in a similar way."

"Don't," I beg breathlessly, feeling my heart thundering and the hives creeping up my chest. I start to inch my way toward the door, but she's following me.

"Please just hear me out?" she says, her voice thickening with emotion too. "He was only five, and it was a head-on collision, in the rain. I didn't think I would survive losing him, but I did because I talked about it. I wanted desperately to be with him again, even if that meant—"

I break into a run, leaving Summer and the crumpled paper behind as I race down the hall in a panic. Pounding footsteps and what must be my name come from behind, but I can barely hear properly with the drumming in my ear and the sound of my own sobs filling the air.

I turn left in the hall, fumbling with handles, and stumble into the first room that allows me sanctuary from students, teachers, my friends . . . everyone.

In the corner of the classroom, I gasp for air, ripping my jean jacket off as I fall to my knees.

I had my first anxiety attack in almost three years the night Mama and Daddy died. My vision blurred at the sight of our totaled van on the screen, and then I saw Ari and Zion run out of Salinger's and into the rain. But I couldn't move my feet. I couldn't feel my legs. I dropped. Someone must've caught me on my way down, but I only remember feeling like my heart was trying to claw its way out of my chest. I felt like I was sinking and knew then I'd never feel what it was like to breathe freely again—live carefree again. Head pounding, sobs flowing, strangers surrounding . . . and then nothing. I still don't know how I got home that night, but when I came to, I was in my bed. And even as the tears stopped and my breath flowed easily again, I didn't feel remotely calm. I felt numb.

I've been coasting on that feeling since that night.

On my hands and knees, my vision blurs again. I squeeze my eyes shut, shaking my head, but when I open them, it's worse. So I try to stand, hearing my father's voice clear as day: *"There's no air down there, Novah."*

I sway halfway up, and a pair of hands shoot out, steadying me. And there's a powdery scent that doesn't make me want to vomit.

"Here, let's, uh, breathe through it," Mrs. Simion says, steering me back to the floor. "First in. Big breath! Then out. Here, watch my cheeks and copy me. There it is. That's better. C'mon, let's do it a couple more times. Big breath in . . . and out."

I let her guide my breathing in and out until I lose track of time. Until I have a handle on it again. Until my heart rate has the chance to slow.

When she thinks I'm well enough, she helps me stand and puts me in my old chair in her classroom.

I hold the wet paper towel she hands me to my head. "I'm sorry," I pant, glancing up finally and seeing the worried look on Mrs. Simion's sharp brown features. "I didn't realize you were in here when I was . . . escaping."

She sits at the desk next to me. "What were you escaping?"

"The Student Grief Support Group."

"Ah," she says knowingly. "Summer tried to welcome you in?"

"Corner me is more like it," I mutter, dropping the towel. I hunch forward to rest on my knees, blinking repeatedly until my vision clears. "That just came out of nowhere."

"Should I call Ariana?" Mrs. Simion asks, reaching out a hand to touch mine.

"No, don't!" That's the last thing I need. For her to see me like this. As miserable as she's been about our parents, Ariana has never let us see her fall apart. She's always kept it together, much better than the rest of us.

I could do the same, and I have been. Even if I had to put in more effort than she ever did. Even if it was a front. "I don't want to bother her at the shop. I'm fine, I just need . . ."

"What, Novah?"

I'm at a loss for words. What do I need? Saying that I need Mama and Daddy back seems childish. It's impossible, and I've already accepted that. Do I need to go home—take the day? No. I won't be able to pick the kids up on their first day of school, and they need me there. Do I need to take off this afternoon? No. If I miss my shift, I throw off the entire schedule.

The bell rings, signaling fifth period. "Nothing," I whisper. "I just need to get myself together."

Mrs. Simion's head cocks to the side, and she holds up a hand, making me pause as I try to stand. "I'll tell you if you don't know. What you need is a moment and I'm giving it to you— No, ma'am, I don't wanna hear it. I'll write your excuse now. It's the first day and no one's gonna be teaching anything anyways. I'll turn the light off, go back to my desk to work, and you take the period to rest yourself."

I open my mouth to retort, but she raises a finger, silencing me.

"Novah, you're tired. I've been where you are before. Parents gone, money to earn, mouths to feed, and adults surrounding me with little to give other than a push to keep moving forward instead of an offer of grace. What you get from me today, and any other day you think you need it, is grace. Go ahead and put your head down," she commands. "I'll wake you before the next bell."

CHAPTER 7

Bailey's marker shoots across her whiteboard before showing us an impressively drawn thumbs-down as our most recent applicant—a freckle-faced man with no grooming experience and what he described as a "mild allergy to dogs"—slumps out of the shop, sneezing into crumpled tissues.

"I *hate* this," Zion grumbles, sitting sprawled in his chair. "I mean, who comes in to interview for a job to literally cut dog hair when they're allergic to dog hair? And what was with that guy who kept going on and on about his preference for cats?" Suddenly he snaps to attention in his seat, hands clasped, hazel eyes wide and begging, "Novah, please make them give me my phone back. I won't text her, I swear!"

I roll my eyes. He's been begging for his phone since I took it this morning.

"Never, ever, never," Miles laughs with his head thrown back like the villain in his favorite cartoon. The Australian shepherd in Bailey's lap wags his tail as she flips her board to show the lone word "lie" scrawled in purple letters.

"See. Even Bailey knows you're a liar and Miles will never give it up, because I promised him vanilla ice cream with hot fudge to hide it."

"And a cookie?" he asks, climbing into my lap.

I nod. "Zi, come on. Your one-sided text thread was giving me secondhand embarrassment. If Isabella says you guys are over, then that's it."

He throws the clipboard with our interview questions to the floor in frustration, making Bailey jump and the puppy yelp. "But why? She won't tell me why!"

I nudge his shoulder with mine, softening my tone. "You know why."

Not that I'd know from experience, but every high school movie will tell you that teen relationships are purposed for spontaneous make-out sessions, sneaking around behind your parents' backs, and fun whirlwind experiences that you randomly think of far past the relationship's expiration. And that's what Isabella and Zion were before. But it became less of the joy of a roller-coaster teen romance and more of a three-month-long mourning fest with no clear end in sight.

Her last text had read: *It's just that you're sad all the time now and I don't know how to cheer you up anymore. I think we should call it quits.*

I was pissed at Isabella for breaking Zion's heart, but I get it. Zi did too. Those sad days broke down into sad hours, minutes, and seconds. Hearing people who have never had their worlds flipped upside down try and empathize with "I know how you're feeling" didn't help. Our neighbors, teachers, friends—none of them really knew what this felt like, and eventually people stopped checking in with us. Eventually casseroles and cakes stopped rolling in. Eventually people had to get on with their lives. And some of them chose to get on without us. Isabella was part of that crew.

And wasn't it better to know anyways?

"Plus, this isn't so bad, Zi," I say, picking up the scattered papers. "I mean, those last two guys were duds, but we know we're gonna hire Taylor—the one with the pretty smile. They've worked as a dog groomer before and they were really nice. And Brent, the guy Jason recommended, will be perfect in the day care rooms. All we need now is to hire one other person for reception, and that's just a part-time position."

"Well, where are we gonna find someone?" Zion says, still pouting. "Allergy guy was our last interview."

"He was the last person who applied online, but Kedijah said she was talking to a kid at school who seemed interested and sounds like a quick learner." I shift Miles off my lap and stretch my legs. "I'm gonna run to the bathro—"

The bell rings before I'm completely out of my seat, and I nearly fall over in surprise. One look at Hailee walking in with a crossbody bag and curious eyes is enough to make me lose complete control of my knees.

"Hey, can we help you?" Zion barely glances her way as he grabs the clipboard.

"Yeah," she says, her voice light and airy. "A girl from school told me about a part time front desk job here, so I thought I'd check it out. Novah, I didn't know this was your family's shop."

I feel goose bumps on the back of my neck rise at the sound of my name on her lips, and make a mental note to buy Kedijah the biggest box of Blue Raspberry Sour Punch Straws I can find.

"Mm-hmm," I say, finding my voice and determining then and there that she has the job. If she's willing to forget our past few awkward encounters, I'm more than happy to follow her lead. "Lively Pups is ours. Uh, and that's my baby brother and sister, Bailey and Miles." Bailey uses the gray, light brown, and white puppy's paw to wave, while Miles belts out an embarrassingly loud "helloooooo" like he's on someone's stage. I roll my eyes, but Hailee giggles. "And this is my brother Zion. He'll be helping run your interview."

She shakes Zion's hand before taking her seat and handing him her résumé.

61

"This should be quick and easy," Zion says, giving her résumé a cursory glance. "Can you tell us a little about yourself, your experience, and why you'd like to work here?"

"Of course. I'm sixteen, and in eleventh grade at Hamer High with Novah—so hopefully that gives me bonus points," Hailee says, waggling her arched brows. "Before last January, I was down in Georgia with my sister and helping out with her hair shop, answering phones, filing some paperwork, and helping out with scheduling too. Now I'm up here with my dad and our two boxers, French and Fry."

She hands me her phone and the screen saver shows one black and one dark brown boxer sitting on either side of Hailee's feet as she leans forward on her knees, smiling broadly.

"Your hair is different," I say, taking the phone and zooming in on the long, spiraled curls she wore in the photo.

Hailee's head falls back. "Ugh. I get the whole love-your-hair movement, but I was hot all the time and my sister wouldn't let me cut it, so as soon as I moved up here, I chopped it all off."

The pixie cut she sported last school year has grown out to coiled curls just passing her full cheeks but not quite reaching her chin. The tiny sparkling nose piercing in her right nostril is new too. And the

September sun has warmed her skin to a beautifully even tone reminiscent of Kelly Rowland's.

"Do you think it's cute? My sister hates it."

"It's definitely cute," I chuckle nervously, shifting in my seat. Hailee smiles with her lips pursed, looking me up and down, before I realize Zion's still there, holding back a smirk himself.

I grab the résumé in his hand, forcing my eyes off her. "Um. Everything sounds really great. I think we can offer—"

"Wha— Wait, Novah!" Zion says with raised brows. "Last question, why do you want to work here?"

Before she can answer, the bell rings and Ari walks in balancing bags of dog food on a giant brown box reading PETGUARD LEASH on the side. "Zi, can you help me?" Miles runs to her aid too, taking a smaller package from her hands before she places a kiss on his forehead.

My shoulders slump just a bit at the sight of Ari. We'd agreed not to fight in front of the kids anymore, but neither of us actually apologized after the Mrs. Lucas blowout—not that I was in the wrong in the first place. My eyes don't leave Hailee's résumé as I say, "We can't use those leashes. They're on Daddy's banned list."

Ari's brows furrow as she pulls out one of the retractable leashes, holding it up for us all to see.

"Why? We need extra leashes for the day care rooms and these were on sale, so I bought them in bulk."

I grimace, moving to the counter with them. "In bulk?! How many did you get?"

"Just, like, fifty," she says, unconcerned.

I exhale as Zion shakes his head. If she'd been at the shop more when Mama and Daddy were running things, she'd know these things. "Retractable leashes are dangerous for dogs. The leash is thin," I say, pulling it out from the handle.

"And if you retract it when the dog is too far away," Zion chimes in, "it can cause severe burns, cuts, or the leash could snap. How many customers do you think would return after someone here accidentally cuts their dog?"

Ari looks between Zion and me, like she's trying to guess if we're playing some trick on her. Her voice comes out small. "How do y'all know all that?"

"It's literally on the poster in Daddy's office on the No Buy List," I say curtly. It was such a waste of money we don't have. And to top it all off, they were on sale and we can't return them. I can see this exact thought running through Ari's head as she looks down at the order form she's holding and folds it in half so we won't see what number is beside the dollar sign.

"Ari, we can't afford to make mistakes like that," Zion says, stating the obvious. "We already had a close call last month not making the mortgage, and Mr. Acosta isn't gonna give me any more advances."

He's right. If we don't start hitting our targets, we'll lose the shop and put Ari's custody arrangement in jeopardy.

Ari runs a hand down her face, and I think we're about to get a rare apology, but a soft bark comes from behind us and Ari's eyes snap up.

"Ooh, don't tell me that dog's owner still hasn't picked him up." She frowns at the puppy still curled in Bailey's lap as she gathers her passion twist in a high ponytail.

"Nope," I sigh. "I called again and still no answer."

"So what do we do with him?" Zion asks.

Ari shrugs. "Well, technically he's been abandoned. I think we should contact a shelter."

A strangled sound emits from Bailey's throat as she hugs the dog's neck with her eyes squeezed shut as if she can't bear the thought. And then her desperate eyes find mine.

I cross the room, bending down where Bailey and the dog sit, and pet his head like I've done at least a hundred times since he was left here a week ago. My hand immediately sinks into his soft fur, and when he nips playfully at my fingers, I scratch behind his floppy gray ears. Every now and then, there's a particular dog brought to the shop that I favor, but since they always leave, I've taught myself not to get too attached. But Bailey is right. This dog is different and still a puppy at six months. We could help him.

"Why . . . don't we keep him?" I say, just floating the idea. I can see anger flash in Ari's eyes at the mere suggestion. Saying it out loud in front of Bailey and Miles makes her the bad guy if she has to say no. But this wasn't me trying to do that.

I stand straight, holding my hands up in defense. "Just hear me out. He barely barks, he's already potty trained, and I checked his files this morning and now I know why his presence is so calming."

"Why?" Ari asks flatly.

"He's been trained as an emotional support dog. I didn't think of it until just now, but he may be a great addition to our family."

Zion crosses his arms over his chest, contemplating. "Hmm. Don't you think he might get a bit over-whelmed in our house?"

"Exactly," Ari agrees. "Plus, we don't need another thing to feed and take care of."

Bailey jumps up, pointing wildly at herself with "me" written on her board, and soon Miles and the puppy join her.

Ari's exhale is ragged as she walks over, bending at the knee in front of Bailey and Miles. "You what, Bails?" Bailey turns the board, grabbing at the dangling mini purple dry-erase pen, but Ari places a hand over hers, smiling gently up at her. "With words?"

The excited smile falls from Bailey's face as her head gives an exaggerated dip to her chest. I know Ari thought that if she could get Bailey to talk, it might make the custody hearing in five months swing in our favor, but this isn't the way to get her there.

The Australian shepherd is at Bailey's feet, whimpering for her attention before her first sniffle can sound. But once I hear it, it feels like the fire that just filled Ari bounds into me, and I move toward her as she straightens with her arms crossed.

Zion steps between us, arms out, speaking firmly like he'd done a million times this summer. "Bailey's speech therapist said trying to force her to speak is the opposite of helpful right now, Ari. You know she's sensitive," he says before turning to me. "Nov, you shouldn't have brought it up in front of them. You're both wrong. So just let it go."

Ari nods, but I'm not ready to let up. I point to Bailey, seated with the puppy nudging his nose to hers, and then at her tearstained cheeks. "Apologize," I urge.

She rolls her eyes, looking toward Zion for a way out, but he agrees with me. "I—I didn't mean to—" and then she looks toward Bailey, deflating as guilt fills her eyes. "I wasn't trying to hurt her feelings." When Ari bends again, she pulls Bailey to her lap, hugging her waist. "Bails, I'm sorry, okay? You can take as much time as you need." Bailey nods at her, wiping at her face, with just the hint of a smile as she raises her head to peck Ari's cheek. And then the puppy is trying to wedge himself between them, this time trying to cuddle up to Ari. And to our surprise, she lets him.

"See," Zion says, leaning on his chair. "The poor thing's gonna be exhausted. We're like an emotional-stability wasteland."

I scowl at him, wanting to be mad, but it's true. Still, even if the puppy ended up working to try and stabilize any of our wild emotions, he'd still get twice as much love from us. There'd be balance.

A phone dings behind me and I'm horrified, turning slowly to see Hailee still there, but her eyes are on her phone screen.

"I'm so sorry! I completely forgot we were in the middle of your interview," I say, grabbing for the clipboard and her résumé, but she's standing.

"No. It's fine," she says, her eyes dodging back and forth between me and the screen. "But my dad was expecting me home so I can meet his date, and now he's blowing up my phone. I should get going."

"No problem," Zion says. "We'll give you a call to let you know our decision."

Before Hailee can exit, she pauses, looking back at

us. "Um, to answer your last question, Zion. I'd love to work here because I have experience as a reception-ist, I absolutely adore dogs, and I can already tell there's a tremendous amount of love here that you can usually only find in these intimate family-owned businesses. I'd love it if I could be a part of one again."

Hailee turns to leave again, but Ari says, "One sec," still cooing in the dog's face. "You sound like a great candidate to me."

Zion nods. "Quick vote?"

I proudly give the first "Aye," followed up by each of my siblings, and Hailee beams.

"We'll email you with your onboarding info," I say. "Can you start next week?"

She nods, before bounding out the door.

I turn, filled with the foreign urge to bear-hug Ari, but she's on her back giggling with the puppy on top of her. I join them on the floor, petting his soft fur, and in one second he's licking at my fingers. The next he's taken off running around us in a circle.

"Bailey's right, Ari," I say. "He's so sweet, and I've seen him make each of us feel better." I laugh, watch-ing him chase Miles around now. "I'm sorry for bringing it up in front of them, but—"

"What should we name him?" Ari interrupts. She smiles—each white tooth showing—and for a second, I'm certain Mama's in here with us.

Bailey scribbles on her little board, pauses, erases, and writes again. She flips it and "POWDER" is written in capital letters.

"Powder it is," Zion says, before scooping Miles up, holding him high in the air, and begging, "Please tell me where my phone is."

CHAPTER 8

I plug my phone into the charger and finally climb in Mama and Daddy's bed, careful not to wake Bailey as she snores with a thumb in her mouth. It just makes more sense to sleep here instead of waking up to Miles, Bailey, or Dante crammed in my twin-sized bed with me. Miles and Dante more often climb in bed with Zion or Ari, but Bailey made this a nightly occurrence. I lucked out on that front. Miles is a serial bed wetter, and Dante's night terrors are enough to make you wanna jump out of your skin. Bailey, on the other hand, sleeps like a rock. A rock that snores like a grown man, but a rock nonetheless.

I glance at the clock. It's 10:30, and I literally have no idea where Ari and Zion are, but all homework's been done—even most of mine—baths have been taken, and all the kids are in bed, and I'm too exhausted to care. I turn on the TV, rushing to lower the volume before it can disturb Bailey, and flip to Channel 4. It never really matters to me what news anchors are talking about; it's their confidence, assuredness, and professionalism that draw me in. In my wildest dreams, I'd get to be in their position, which is probably why the late-night news has always lulled me to sleep. Trinity Dawson pops up in her back-length braids and a bright red blazer, speaking about some politician's sex scandal, and I settle in.

My phone vibrating on the nightstand five minutes later jolts me out of my daze, and I fully expect a text from my friend group chat, but an unknown number brightens the screen.

> Hey, it's Hailee! I got your number from the email you sent. Sorry to be texting so late!

I sit up straight, suddenly feeling the happy thumps of my heart in my chest, and then another message pops up.

> **Hailee:** I know I'm not on the schedule to start until next Monday, but I'm free tomorrow if you guys need an extra hand at reception

> **Novah:** That would actually be perfect. Your training should take less than a day

> **Hailee:** Sounds good. I'll be there right after school

> **Hailee:** Question. Who's training me?

Novah: *I've been covering afternoon reception this past week. So probably me*

Hailee: *Oh okay*

Hailee: *Awesome! Can't wait!*

Novah: *See you then!*

I settle into bed, holding a pillow close to my chest as the TV plays in the background. But I don't need to listen to their words tonight. Those few texts from Hailee alone give me all the comfort I need.

◊◊◊

Distant, pained, and terrified screeches jolt me awake along with Bailey's foot jutting into my ribs. I scramble to untangle myself from the blankets acting as a strait-jacket, but the wet sheets beneath me force me to pause. Did I . . . ? No, of course not.

"Ugh," Bailey moans in disgust, sitting up in the wet too.

I rip the blankets off us in the king-sized bed to reveal the culprit beside me, still asleep, despite Dante's ongoing shrieks down the hall. Another night terror.

"Miles," I groan groggily, placing my feet on the

cold, hard floor in search of my slippers, "you wet the bed again."

He sits up too, naked from the waist down and wiping at crust in his eyes. "Nuh-uh."

A light switches on in the hall, and I see just a flash of Ari, then Korey rushing toward Dante's room. Powder's barking behind the doggy gate at the foot of the stairs. And right on cue, banging from behind the wall.

"Shut that noise up. It's one in the mornin'," yells Mr. Crane's muffled voice.

I let my face fall into my hands at the edge of the bed, giving an audible groan at the thought of the bags that'll surely be under my eyes in the morning. And I can't help but think how none of this would be happening if Mama and Daddy were here right now.

Easily defeated, I collapse on the bed to a disturbing squish and pop right back up again with my back covered almost entirely in pee. This is the fifth time in two weeks.

An hour later, I come down the stairs freshly showered in an oversized Ari Lennox T-shirt to hear the washer and dryer knocking. There are dim lights on in the living room. The soft croons of H.E.R. play from our old radio as Dante still sniffles with Powder snuggling in his lap. Bailey and Miles flank him with equally tired expressions.

"Night diaper stays on if you're gonna get in bed with us, Miles. That's the rule," I say, shuffling into the kitchen, just as Ari emerges from the laundry room, her pink bonnet askew.

"We're gonna have to get the dryer looked at again," she says, glancing back at it nervously. "I don't think it's supposed to make that sound, and it's gonna take forever for the comforter to dry."

I grab a bottle of water from our near-empty fridge and scan the chore chart. It's Zion's turn to go grocery shopping, and I gotta remember to take the trash out in the morning. "I'll call Mr. Johnston tomorrow, but what are we gonna do about Dante?" My exaggerated whisper is rendered useless by a particularly rowdy new round of knocking coming from the dryer.

Ari shakes her head. "I don't know anymore. We've tried the sleepy-time tea and gummies; the bath salts before bed didn't work; the night light is useless. I mean—the night terrors are basically every other night at this point, and it's getting harder to wake him up, and now we have the barking dog too. I'm just surprised Mr. Crane hasn't called the cops on us yet."

"Oh, it's definitely coming," Korey says, descending the steps with his durag and Naruto pajama pants on. He slumps into the chair, laying his big head in his hand.

"Maybe I can swing by the store and get him a

'thanks for tolerating us' gift basket in the morning and fill it with beef jerky."

"Who cares about Mr. Crane?" I ask, annoyed.

"We all should," Ari says, wringing a dry dish towel nervously. "What if Ms. Lusby decides to ask him how he thinks things are going during one of her surprise drop-ins? She doesn't even know about Dante's night terrors, and all he hears is a child screaming his lungs out every night. Do you really think that cranky old man is gonna say anything helpful about us?"

Ugh, I hadn't thought of that. Ms. Lusby is by no means cruel, but she is way too strict, in my opinion.

"Or what if he personally puts in a call to Child Protective Services? Who knows what Ms. Lusby or even the judge will do? I mean, we know we're all better with each other, but they're still making that decision. We have to placate Mr. Crane at least until the custody hearing in January, right?"

The three of us exchange nervous looks. The word *separation* floats unspoken between us. The reminder—fear, really—of foster care has me searching for options.

"I think that store Franky and Lou over in Bowie had jerky and cheese gift baskets."

Ari nods. "And what about Dante? Before we could calm him down, he just kept saying 'The hearing, the hearing.' I mean, I know he's worried about January. We all are. But maybe it's time to get some outside help. Should we try to get him a therapist or something? The judge said they'd be available at our request."

Korey shakes his head. "Won't that just be telling them that we don't know what we're doing?"

"Or maybe it'll show them that we're really trying and willing to ask for help when we need it." I look back at Dante petting Powder with one hand. Bailey's holding his other, and my chest tightens. I'd never seen this look on his face before Mama and Daddy passed, and now it's getting to be normal. "He just looks so sad."

"Zion always knows how to cheer him up," Ari says. "What's he doing upstairs?"

Korey shrugs. "Not here."

"What?"

"He's not in our room, Ari. I just checked everywhere. He either has the power of invisibility now or he's not here."

I glance at the clock. It's 2:18 a.m.

Just as Ari and I pull out our phones to call, keys jingle at the door, and a second later, Zion walks in with a purpling bruise on his left cheek and squinting eyes full of confusion.

"Why is everyone up?"

"Dante was screaming again," Miles says, bounding into his arms.

"And Miles wet the bed again," Dante spits, jumping out of his seat too.

"Fight?" Bailey signs.

Korey and Ari follow me out of the kitchen as I walk up to Zion, examining his cheek. "Chris?" I ask.

"I told that asshole, it was on sight when I saw him."

"Who is Chris?!" Ari yells, confused.

"Isabella's new boyfriend," Korey answers, snickering.

Ari shakes her head, annoyed. "Zi, it's really late. We agreed you'd be home before eleven thirty, *not* waltzing in after two, smelling like weed and beat up."

"I was home by eleven thirty, and then he started texting my phone looking for a fight and he found one."

"Did you at least win?" I ask, and Ari nudges my elbow.

"Not before he got in a few good shots." He puts Miles down, playfully boxing with him for a second. We all follow him into the kitchen, where he finds an old bag of broccoli florets in the freezer and slaps it on his face. Soon his eyes find Dante's across the table. "Rough night for you too?"

Dante nods, casting his eyes down at his fingers.

Ari bends at his side, brushing his baby locs to the side. "What can we do to help, buddy?"

He shrugs.

"Did you try the tea-and-white-noise combo we talked about?" Zion asks.

"Didn't help," he mumbles.

"Well, these night terrors are worse than I remember," Korey says, scratching his head, "but this isn't the first time he's had them. What would Mama do?"

His question acts as a light switch, and suddenly the bulb is on. I exit the kitchen, pass Powder lounging on his bed, and head straight to the altar. I look at Daddy for a moment but stare straight into Mama's eyes in the frame.

When Dante was a toddler, he had similar night terrors. Korey was right: These night terrors are worse because they're fueled by the trauma of losing our parents. Mama would probably handle them with the spiritual aids she always used to calm us when we were younger. To cleanse us and our space and to center us. So far, only Korey's kept up with her practices like we all should. He refills the water in the glass goblet on the altar once a day, sages our home at least once a week, and always kneels at the altar to speak, pray, think, and petition, often pulling Miles and Bailey to their knees with him.

I sit at the foot of the altar now, pulling the big decorated polka-dot gray box near me and flipping open the lid. Inside is her Bible, sage, bottles of Florida water cologne, palo santo sticks, old journaling books, brown paper bags, tall candles, herbs, and oils.

Within the hour, every inch of the house has been

cleansed. We open the windows, telling Dante that every bit of bad energy has been expelled, and follow up by using the Florida water on ourselves just like Mama used to do to us—a drop or two of the cologne rubbed in her hands before wiping down the back of our necks, with a dab at our cheeks.

It's Zion who finds the handwritten guide and the crystals she had to stash away when Miles began trying to eat them like candies. They were in Mama and Daddy's room, stored in an old hatbox in the corner of her closet.

"I came in here maybe a week before the accident and she was working on them," Zion says, digging through the hatbox with a gleam in his eye. "I completely forgot, but she said she was almost done, and it looks like she finished." He pulls out seven bracelets. Each holding our initial and crystals she must've thought best aligned with us.

Ari hands them out, putting her rose quartz bracelet to the side. A hematite bracelet for Zion, amazonite for Korey, black tourmaline for Dante, Angelite for Bailey, citrine for Miles. And then she hands me the tiger's-eye bracelet with a silver *N* charm hanging in the middle.

I slide my bracelet on my left wrist and run my shaky fingers over the smooth brown crystals. According to the guide, the tiger's-eye crystal represents willpower and self-motivation, helps to release anxiety, and aids harmony.

It was a gift from Mama—even after her ascension. I wonder if she knew when crafting just how much we'd want them. Just how much they'd calm and center us. Or even how much we'd need them, especially in her physical absence. I promise her to never take it off.

CHAPTER 9

"Okay, so the key to the filing cabinets stays in this drawer. Oh, and I think I misplaced your script," I say, looking around the cluttered reception desk. Hailee's scanning the desk too when I spot the pink laminated paper under a binder. But when I reach for it, she does too, and our hands brush before I pull back as if I've been stung.

"Whoops, I'm sorry!" she says, smiling feebly at me.

I shake my head. "No, it was me. It was a late night, and I'm just a bit jumpy." I reach for the paper again without embarrassing myself this time. "So, you just need to—"

Bailey clears her throat at the little desk in the waiting room, and I excuse myself.

Powder sits at her feet, panting with his little tongue out, only occasionally popping his head up at the chorus of barks coming from the back room. "Your marigolds look perfect, Bai," I say, looking at the flowers she's drawn in her little sketch pad. I bend beside her to pet Powder. "What's up? You hungry?"

"Yes," she signs. "And you have to be calm. Feel your bracelet." She points at the tiger's-eye crystal on my wrist.

I look back at Hailee, but she's distracted, alphabetizing client forms.

"Is it that obvious?" I whisper, and she grimaces with a nod.

I stand, wiping my sweaty palms on my yellow work shirt, and go back to my seat with Powder resting at my feet now.

"Right, so the script is pretty straightforward," I say, twisting the crystals on my bracelet between my fingers. "Literally read it word for word and, uh, eventually, it should be as easy to rattle off as your address."

"Actually," Hailee says with a little smile, "I already know it by heart. I had some time last night and just thought I'd try and make a good impression." She turns to watch as Bailey giggles at something on her screen.

Hailee points toward the white ASL basic signs poster on the wall. "How long have you all been using ASL?"

I'd forgotten that sign was there, but I'm grateful to talk about something outside of work. "Only for, like, four years. We learned because of Bailey."

"Is it weird for me to ask why?"

"Well, we've known Bailey was on the spectrum

since she was one, and in case she grew up to be non-speaking, my mama signed us all up for ASL classes. Eventually, she stuttered her first word, *flower*, at three, when they were gardening one day. But that's how she primarily communicates."

Hailee cocks her head to the side curiously. "Was it hard to actually learn?"

"Probably as hard as it is to learn most languages. But we were all determined. Why? Are you thinking about taking ASL in school?"

She nods. "I dunno when I'll end up using French, and ASL seems more practical."

"Well . . . if you do decide to switch over, I'll be happy to help."

Hailee's doe eyes widen. "Are you sure? I was kind of starting to feel like you might not—" The phone rings, and the gold bangles on her wrists clatter as her hands shoot out to answer. "Oh, I can practice the script!" She clears her throat and lifts the receiver.

"Hello, this is Hailee speaking at Lively Pups, where we make all your pup's day care, grooming, and boarding dreams come true. How can I help you this afternoon?"

I throw her a thumbs-up.

"Okay. Yeah, of course. I'll be sure to let everyone know that Jason can't come in today because his daughter is sick."

My head falls back in annoyance. Other than Antoinette, Jason is our most consistent employee now. And considering Zion and Ari were both late (as usual), I really needed him.

"I guess I'm gonna have to train Korey today. And miss the career fair too," I say, bummed. I heard a rumor at school that Trinity Dawson would be there. Lila Vance was my favorite news anchor for so long, but after recent events, I found it really hard not to change the channel whenever I saw her face. Dawson, on the other hand, is a Hamer alum and brings a fresh, new energy to every segment she hosts. I'm sure nothing would come out of it, but it still would've been nice to actually meet her.

I don't have time to sulk, because a second later, our eyes snap up when the bell rings. In comes Antoinette, trailed by a regular named Jerry with his drooly leashed Doberman, Lulu. And a girl no older than twelve, holding an obviously used chew toy in one hand and a receipt in the other.

"My class got canceled, so I thought I'd come give a hand," Antoinette says, shouting over Powder and Lulu, who are alternating between barking and trying to sniff each other's butts. Antoinette just barely catches Bailey as she jumps into her arms, and I feel the weight lift off my shoulders when Hailee immediately helps Jerry, while Antoinette handles the little girl. I may not be able to ever really count on Ari showing up when I need her, but Antoinette never fails. I hope I can grow to count on Hailee like that too—at least as an employee.

◊◊◊

In the washroom, I lean over the edge of the deep silver bathtub in my waterproof apron to guide the soapy goldendoodle back toward me.

"That's a good boy, Teddy," I schmooze in the old dog's face, lathering the last of the soap down the bridge of his nose, careful to avoid his eyes. "Okay, so tell me the big steps up until this point again."

Korey sighs from a stool behind me with his face in his phone. "Put 'em in the tub, use the suction leash if they're agitated or squirrelly, pre-brush, apply shampoo—"

"What about soaking?"

"That's not obvious?"

I grab the faucet and begin rinsing Teddy as he tries to squirm away from the stream. "Not if I have to ask. No."

"Soak the dog, apply shampoo—"

"Starting where?"

"At the legs and work my way up," he huffs. "Are you gonna let me finish or keep interrupting me every two seconds? 'Cause I already know how to do this. It's a waste of time."

I pause rinsing Teddy's legs and glare back at Korey. "Dude, your attitude is on ten today. You had a bad day at school or something?"

Silence.

"Well, I've had a few bad parts since school started up too, but at least it's Friday."

He hops off his stool, leaning on the tub beside me. Just last year, I had at least three inches on him. Now we're eye to eye, and his eyes are worried. "Bad like the anxiety attack?"

I swallow hard and grab the towel, just so I can have something else to look at. My anxiety attack was undoubtedly the worst part of the last two weeks, but I didn't want Korey to know about that. He shouldn't have to worry about me. I didn't want any of them to doubt I was holding it together.

But Monae told Zion about my little freak-out in the cafeteria on Monday. He showed up in Mrs. Simion's classroom five minutes before the bell rang and I made him promise not to tell Ari, but I should've covered all my bases.

I was grateful for the forty-five minutes Mrs. Simion was able to give me, but the recovery after one of those attacks was an all-day type of thing. I fell asleep in Mr. Lane's class afterward and he wasted no time yelling at me in front of the whole class. Zion offered to pick up the kids and skip out on his shift at Acosta's, but I was still so foggy at work that I messed up two returns and tried to give a new customer the wrong Chihuahua.

I bite the inside of my cheek. "Heard about that, huh?"

He nods. "That's the second one. What does it feel like?"

"Like . . . I'm dying in slow motion but everything around me is happening at warp speed. It sucks."

Korey takes the towel from me, allowing Teddy to hop on the edge to lick his face before drying him off. "It *was* a bad day. I told Mr. Jenkins to go . . ." His eyes dart around the room as he searches for the words. ". . . pleasure himself."

I open my mouth. Close it and open it again. "Why would you do that?"

"He kept bugging me about not paying attention when I was, and then said something about me barely making it to the eighth grade in front of the whole class." He avoids my eyes and opens the tub door, letting Teddy hop down onto the mat. "You don't have to say anything. I already know I was wrong and I already told Ari since she had to sign the slip. It was actually kinda scary," he says, leaning on the tub beside me, looking spooked. "You know she has those eyes that bulge out when she's pissed just like Daddy."

I bark a laugh, removing my apron when he starts imitating the action.

He bends to leash Teddy, but when he looks up, his eyes are serious. "Ari was saying that any of us failing classes this year could really affect whether we get to stay with each other?"

"Yeah?"

"Do you think that's true? Or was she just trying to scare me straight?"

I bite the inside of my cheek, toying with the answer, because maybe he deserves that kid-like innocence. But lying when it very well could count against us doesn't help any of us. Just as I'm about to open my mouth, Hailee bursts in, in a panic. "Novah, they need help with Peaches in one of the day care rooms!"

She runs out, and we follow her through the grooming door. A sudden crash and distressed voices come clearer in the hallway holding our three day care rooms, where Miles stands pinching his nose. Bailey looks disgusted and points toward the middle door.

Day care room two, our holding center for medium-sized dogs, is in chaos. Antoinette's teetering around, careful of where she steps in the grassy playroom, attempting to get four of the remaining free dogs into their cages. Dante's in the corner gagging. Taylor looks like they're gonna be sick too, as they chase Peaches, the labradoodle, around, trying to get her in one spot. And the smell is rancid. I wanna run back out, but Korey beats me to it.

"She has diarrhea," Taylor yells. "And every time she finishes in one spot, she runs to the next!"

Hailee tiptoes past several piles of shit in the grass, toward Taylor and Peaches, while I push Dante out. And then I'm chasing the free dogs too.

An hour later, I'm on my hands and knees with a face mask on, scrubbing the last remnants of Peaches's mess out of a mat. Hailee's across the room, rubbing the exhausted dog's stomach. Earlier, Taylor, being new, let Dante convince them that he knew what and how to feed all the dogs, not considering Peaches's allergy to soy. Luckily this didn't turn into an emergency veterinary situation, but Antoinette reminds me of how bad it could've been when she gets off the phone with her owners. They're on the way.

I stand, stripping my gloves off, and notice the stains on Hailee's jeans.

"Hey, I have some spare clothes in my dad's office if you wanna change before your shift ends."

She nods eagerly and leads Peaches, who looks much more content, into her cage before following me out.

Daddy's office is mostly how he left it. The old desk still holds a stress ball in the shape of a dog bone, scattered papers, and the screen saver on his desktop is a candid of the nine of us at Thanksgiving dinner two years ago. There's a basketball hoop hung on the back of his door, and all his certificates are framed on the walls around us. I go to the fourth filing cabinet and open the drawer with my name scribbled on the label.

"Since we're here a lot more than we used to be, Ari thought it would be nice for all of us to have a space where we keep a few spare items."

"Why don't you guys use the lockers the rest of the staff does?" she asks, straightening a photo of Mama and Daddy hanging on the paneled wall.

I chuckle, pulling out two pairs of black shorts and a choice between an old tie-dye Lively Pups shirt or a *Bob's Burgers* graphic tee. "Those lockers are gonna come crashing down any day now. If you ever have something important, I can put it in here. Which shirt?" I ask, turning around, holding up the options.

Hailee takes a step back, surveying them with a finger to her chin and a scrutinizing eye. And then points at the graphic tee.

I pucker my bottom lip in approval. "Good taste. There's a bathroom right there."

When she closes the door behind her, I strip off my stained clothes and clumsily step into the shorts, proud that I avoided embarrassing myself for an entire five minutes in front of her. As long as I can keep that night out of my head, I can pretend to be a normal person.

"I bet you didn't think your first day would end like this, huh," I shout apologetically while pulling on my shirt. "I thought Taylor was gonna pass out for a second there."

Hailee walks out, pulling her short hair up in a ponytail. "Oh, that was nothing; once French and Fry got into my Halloween stash and ate half the chocolate before I caught them. The mess they made . . ." She pulls herself up on the desk next to me, and I force myself to stay put, even though it feels like my heart's leapt into my throat. "My dad had to replace all the carpet, and it took *months* for his house to smell normal again. It's funny now, but I thought he was gonna kill me when he got home."

I pretend to gag. "Oh god, that's awful."

We're quiet for a moment, legs swinging and staring at the wall, when Hailee looks nervous suddenly.

"Don't tell me," I chuckle anxiously, "you had a change of mind and wanna turn in your work shirt already?"

She smirks, and then her lips bunch seriously at one side. "No, it's not that. I think I'm gonna love it here. It's just . . . I keep thinking about that day at Acosta's. You remember it, right?"

My eyes drop, and I find myself scraping at the polish on my thumb, but I summon enough nerve to nod.

"When you saw me, you turned to leave so fast, you accidentally made a display of oranges fall. And I don't know why, but I couldn't get the image out of my head all summer. I thought I did something to upset you, and that maybe you'd never wanna be bothered with me again, especially after the first day of school. But you were so nice at my interview, and then it was weird again earlier today, and now it feels . . . I don't know?"

My stomach plummets to my feet. I hate that I've made her feel that way. When I force my eyes up, I find her eyes locked on mine, and suddenly the words that I couldn't even say to my friends come tumbling out. "I was embarrassed by how I reacted that night in Salinger's."

It looks like Hailee's full brows are about to meet her hairline, they fly up so fast. "What? Novah, no, of course not. How could you even worry about that?"

"I know it probably sounds silly, but . . . do you remember the day you asked if I'd be at Salinger's after the volleyball game? I don't know why, but I guess I convinced myself you asked because you might be interested in me. And I just figured after you saw me lose it that night, you wouldn't be interested anymore." My lips purse, and this time my fingers find the cool tiger's-eye crystals around my wrist. "My panic attacks are probably the least attractive thing about me," I try to joke. But Hailee's expression is serious. She hops down from the desk, fully facing me now.

"The first thing you have to know about me is that I'd never judge someone for how they react about losing a parent," she says, holding up a finger. "The second is that I lost my mom when I was eight, so I get what that feels like. And third," she smiles, "Novah, I never lost interest."

My chest swells, and I peek up at her through my lashes, fully showing every tooth as I grin. "Neither did I."

We stare at each other, unmoving, for so long that I jump when her phone dings between us. "Oh, my cousin's been waiting outside for ten minutes." She moves from me, carefully stuffing her dirty clothes into a plastic bag and placing it in her satchel. "I'll, uh—be sure to wash these."

"You can return them whenever, or keep them, it doesn't really matter."

She nods with a smile, but just as her hand's about to touch the door handle, she turns to face me. "Or . . . I could give them back when I see you tomorrow."

"Oh, I don't work tomorrow, and I'm pretty sure you don't either. Hold on, let me check the schedule." I hop down to check Daddy's computer, but Hailee moves and then she's blocking the way.

"I don't," she says lightly, playing with the gold ring

on her middle finger. "I just thought, it's been nice talking to you today. And it would be nicer if we could talk more . . . like when neither of us smells like dog shit," she laughs.

My insides flutter, but I try to play it cool, stuffing my hands into my back pockets. "Yeah. No. Yeah. That would be nice! D-do you wanna maybe meet up somewhere?"

Her coy smirk breaks into a full-fledged smile. "I do! There's this shaved ice pop-up place on Marlboro Pike called Houey's— And, Novah, oh my god! It's delicious. Have you been?"

"No, but I'd love to. I'm free tomorrow, anytime," I say quickly, abandoning the cool act. I wanna be where she is and I want her to know it.

Hailee bounds backward to the door, beaming. "Great, then it's a date! I'll text you tonight."

CHAPTER 10

Novah: *She just flat out asked. And not like last time when we were gonna coincidentally be in the same restaurant. This is a date date!*

Monae: *Oooooh you got a date with her on her first day at work lol that's impressive*

Kedijah: *It's about time! After all that hot and heavy staring last year, I'm surprised it took this long*

Oma: *Call us tonight so we can pick out your outfit*

Novah: *I will around 10!*

I send the last text before locking the door behind us as we leave Lively's. Ari showed up a mere thirty minutes ago—without a single explanation of where she'd been. I'm too annoyed to speak and let Antoinette update Ari on the chaos of the day. That is, until Ari throws me the keys as I head for the passenger door.

"Wait," I say with a slow smile creeping across my face, "are you serious?"

"Yep." Ari clicks Miles's car seat in place before walking around to the passenger side. "I'm exhausted, you have your learner's permit, and you still need a couple of practice hours before your test next month, right? Here's your time to shine."

I know this is her small way of apologizing for bailing on us today, letting me drive ten minutes up the street for our weekly family dinner. I haven't been able to practice much lately. Driving came easy to me when Daddy first started teaching me last year. So I'm not complaining today.

My good mood doesn't last long, though. It's hard to enjoy my short drive with Ari rambling nonstop about some register inconsistencies, and Miles shouting his ABCs at the top of his lungs the whole way there. And things don't calm down much after we reach the restaurant.

I wave our waiter over to our booth in Chickie's Grill and shout over the music to make myself heard. "We asked for the mac and cheese, not the fries, to go with this meal," I say, handing him Bailey's plate, "and his chicken still has a bit of red in it and he won't eat it like that." I grab Dante's untouched plate too and turn to Korey. "Is yours right?"

"Technically, yes," he says grumpily, stabbing at the

green beans on his plate, "but a chef with a clear lack of talent at a three-and-a-half–starred restaurant on Yelp? No, that's not right."

I catch our waiter roll his eyes as he walks away.

"You're such a snob, Korey," Ari says, digging her fork into his salmon and popping it into her mouth. "We haven't found the right restaurant yet, but we will. And it's really important that we have these Friday-night family dinners to keep us all together, outside of work."

Korey sits cross-armed in his seat. "Yeah, well, I liked Salinger's. Their burgers are the best."

"Half of us have vowed never to step foot in Salinger's again," I say, watching Miles like a hawk. I refuse to be stuck finding hidden baby carrots around the house for the next week. "It's not happening. Get over it."

"It's not a full family dinner if Zion's not here," Dante says, sipping from his Sprite.

I exchange a worried look with Ari.

"I'll just call him again." She pulls out her phone, stepping away from the table, I'm sure so she can whisper-yell at him through another voice mail without the kids overhearing.

Ari misses an occasional shift every now and then, but Zion has been downright unreliable lately. This is the second Friday family dinner he's missed this month. The fifth in the last two months. If he's not missing these dinners, then it's his shifts, and if it's not his shifts, he's forgetting his daily chore on the chart. I pull out my phone to shoot him a quick text.

> *You said you'd be here tonight. The foods horrible, but the kids are asking about you*

And then another.

> *I'll get you something to go. A chicken sandwich?*

The table shaking forces my eyes up, and it's Bailey standing in her seat, waving wildly at someone across the restaurant. I look, hopeful to see Zion.

"Dijah! Dijah!" Miles yells, drawing eyes toward us from every direction.

I shush him and pull Bailey down, but wave Kedijah over from the pickup window.

"You doing Uber Eats with your dad again?" I ask.

She nods. "The order's not ready yet, so I have a minute," she says, taking Ari's seat. She pulls Bailey and Miles into her lap as she reads Bailey's board. "I miss you too. We gotta hang out more. Food's gross, huh?" she asks Korey.

"If food is what you wanna call it."

She chuckles as Miles begins pulling her full cheeks and rubbing the fabric of her dark blue hijab. "You gotta new glow about you," she says to me knowingly. "Now that I think about it, Hailee was cheesing nonstop at the career fair too. Where were you?"

I bite my bottom lip, trying to play down my excitement since Dante's eavesdropping ears are all in our conversation. "An employee called in sick, Ari showed up late, Zion never showed up at all, and then one of the dogs had a poop accident because *somebody* decided they wanted to run things." Dante finally looks away with a scowl. "So I got caught up at the shop. Why, did Trinity actually show up?"

"Showed up *and* she was really nice." Kedijah digs in her jacket pocket and hands me a card. "I was gonna give you this on Monday."

My eyes light up. The black card with gold lettering reads TRINITY DAWSON, NEWS ANCHOR/JOURNALIST, with her number, email, and everything. After she graduated from Hamer High, Trinity went on to UNC at Chapel Hill, where she played for three and a half years before suffering a career-ending ACL injury. Luckily, she had her journalism degree to fall back on when her WNBA dreams were squashed. Now she works at the local Channel 4 News as an anchor.

"Ugh, I'm so sad I missed her! But you got her card for me?"

"Not only that, Nov, I was talking you up! And it turns out she knew your dad *way* back when. Something about a rescue dog that had aggressive tendencies. Her parents wanted to give him up until your dad trained and housebroke him. She showed me a picture of her and Ice too. He's this really old spotted pit bull."

"Spotted like a Dalmatian?" Dante asks.

"More like a cheetah."

I wave my hand. "And, and?"

"Oh right! I told her that even though you suck at basketball, you love watching the news, which is weird for a sixteen-year-old, if you ask me. And then I told her about your dream to pursue journalism."

The waiter comes back out with our correct orders, and I move to cut Dante's chicken. "Bails, you gotta let it cool down," I say, and stuff napkins down Miles's shirt like a bib to stop the dribble of fruit punch. I turn back to Kedijah, but Korey asks to be let out of the booth. "What—where are you going?"

"To see if I can talk to the cook," he says, heading for the kitchen.

I roll my eyes, leaning back in the seat before I remember Kedijah's there. "I mentioned being interested in journalism to you once."

"Yeah, once a week!" she scoffs. "Nov, Trinity personally told me to give you her card and said you can call anytime to set up a day to shadow her. And the best part? Drumroll, please . . ."

Miles, Bailey, and Dante begin drumming on the table.

"She's looking for two new interns. Just someone to maybe come in twice a week to learn more about the business."

I feel a jolt of excitement as I envision myself in a sleek black dress and a bright blue blazer reporting the news on TV instead of just watching a screen. But one quick look around the table full of my busy siblings is enough to make the fantasy drift away. How could I take on any new responsibilities right now? I'm gearing up to say no when Ari comes up behind me and snatches the card out of my hands.

"Number eight, Kedijah. Number eight, Kedijah," a server says from the pickup window.

She ignores them.

"And this is, like, a legit internship opportunity?" Ari asks. "Oh, Trinity Dawson, I love her!"

"Yes, it's legit," Kedijah says, standing. "I spoke to her myself. Novah, I know you're busy, but really think about it before you say no. Even just shadowing her could lead to something." She pulls her buzzing phone out of her pocket and holds it to her ear. "I'm coming with the food now, Baba," she says. She hugs me goodbye, waves to the others, and hurries off.

Ari pulls me from the table by my arm with furrowed brows. "That sounds like an amazing opportunity. Why would Kedijah think you'd say no?"

I scoff. "Because I have no choice but to say no. I mean, maybe I could shadow her one day. That'd be nice. But I definitely don't have time to intern with her a couple times a week."

"Says who?"

"Says me."

"And why couldn't you intern with Trinity two or three days out of the week? I mean, you are still a kid, Novah, and kids deserve to pursue their dreams, or at least figure out if it's a dream worth pursuing."

I stare at her in wide-eyed disbelief. "Are you serious?"

"Yeah, why wouldn't I be? We could—"

I shake my head and cut her off. "Ari, stop. You know I literally don't have the time. School is a handful. The shop is a handful. And the kids are two handfuls. I only have two hands."

She chuckles. "I didn't realize you were doing this on your own. You sound like a single mother or something."

"Feels like it sometimes."

Her head cocks to the side. "I'm sorry?"

"Ari, where were you last night when I was helping the kids do homework? I had to do bath time by myself and put them to bed. And where were you this afternoon? I picked up the kids, went to work, and you didn't show up for three hours." I throw my arms up in frustration. "That's why I was stuck there to teach Korey how to wash. That's why I got stuck cleaning up dog shit, and that's why I missed the career fair and couldn't be there to meet Trinity myself. I mean, even if you had bothered to show up on time, we still would've been understaffed because Zion didn't come either. And as you can see, he's also not here. If this was an internship day and I had to choose between the kids and the shop or the internship, guess what I would've had to do?"

She shakes her head. "Novah, if that was the case, we would have worked it out. I mean, we are still kids—"

"No, we're not anymore. Not you. Not Zion. And I can't remember the last time I felt like a kid."

"What is that supposed to mean?" Ari says. The indignation in her voice is enraging. All those years, had she really thought we were all on an equal playing field?

"It means that even when Mama and Daddy were here, you and Zion got to do the fun teenage thing, while I was at the shop or at home being the third parent, Ari. What, do you think I was getting to be a kid any of the hundreds of times you got me to cover so you could hang out with your friends? Look." I pause to take a breath. "The point is that me, you, and Zion aren't kids anymore. And we have no choice but to let that be okay. And it's probably best if we keep the dreams to Korey, Dante, Bailey, and Miles. I wanna exist in reality."

Ari stands in front of me looking sad and confused,

as if she's upset I've lost my childlike wonder. As if I'm the one being stubborn instead of her. Like she has no idea she should be apologizing right now. Apologizing for acting like she always knew best. Apologizing for forcing me to pick up her slack. Apologizing for dangling this dream in my face when we both know it isn't a possibility.

"Well, at least take the card and think about it," she says, holding it out to me. "I think we could make this happen for you. You deserve it if you want it."

Her eyes say she means it, but I'm not that gullible.

A crash behind us makes us jump. Half the plates and drinks that were on our table are now on the floor along with a crying, food-covered Miles. Just like clockwork.

I turn back to Ari and push the card away. "That's what I mean. My dream right now is to make sure we stay together. That card and whatever you're doing behind our backs won't make that happen. Whether you realize it or not, we don't have time for anything else, Ari."

CHAPTER 11

"Miles, you have to at least try to color inside the lines," Ari says, sitting crisscross applesauce next to him on the living room floor.

I peek at them over my copy of *I Know Why the Caged Bird Sings*. I know I should be more focused on my schoolwork considering how behind I am on my reading for English and how unprepared I am for my upcoming history test. But I'm too distracted by Korey cooking behind me, Zion's clicking keyboard, and daydreams of finally getting real alone time with Hailee on our date this afternoon. Hopefully it goes better than it did in my nightmare last night. Dream Hailee ended up leaving our date in a rage when I had to show up with Miles, Bailey, and Dante after Ari, Zion, and Korey went MIA.

"I am," Miles whines, sloppily coloring a branch for his family tree project in his full Spider-Man costume. The cut-out pictures of us lie beside him ready to be glued. Parts of our faces, hair, and heads

106

are cut off or into, but he insisted that "big boys cut alone."

I hold another of Bailey's picture cards up with my other hand, and she correctly spells *apple* before going back to her plain yogurt—the only kind she'll eat.

Antoinette's in charge of the shop today, as we all have Saturday morning off to focus on schoolwork. But I can't focus with my grumbling stomach, so I head over to bug Korey again.

I drop my book, leaning on the back of my chair to gaze at the Belgian waffle he's placing on a plate. "How much longer?" I ask for the third time, licking my lips. Powder's at Korey's feet doing the same.

Korey pours batter into the waffle maker, not bothering to look my way. "It's done when it's done."

Dante bounds into the kitchen with a *National Geographic* magazine in his hands, a smile on his face, and immediately runs up to Korey, speaking a mile a minute about this month's issue. We were all just happy to see him smiling again, and hoping for another night free of his night terrors.

"You're sure you finished all of your work?" Ari asks him.

"It's the first week; all we had was reading and math review, and I already read ahead."

He holds the magazine open to show Korey some prehistoric extinct rhino when Ari shrieks in annoyance. My head swings and I see the mess in action. The rubber cement Miles was holding is somehow all over his costume and sinking into the carpet.

I watch, amused, as Ari turns in a huff to wet a washcloth and returns, dabbing at the cement in the carpet on her hands and knees as she rants to Miles about paying attention. But he's gone full Spider-Man, jumping from the couch to the banister to the floor and Ari's back.

"Don't!" Korey yells as Miles crouches on the armrest and leaps at the TV stand. He grabs on to a high shelf, hanging for just a second, and then lands in a pose that might've been outrageously cute if it weren't for the towering, teetering TV stand about to crush him and Ari. One second Korey's behind me beating eggs, and the next, he's rushing over to the altar but isn't quick enough to keep the offerings, picture frames, or our ancestors' tokens from crashing to the floor.

With a sigh, I join them in the living room and begin cleaning the floor and straightening the altar while Ari tries to drag a wailing Miles toward the steps.

"I can't change! I'm Spider-Man!"

"Well, you gotta be Miles Morales for a few hours, 'cause that needs to go in the wash."

I search the carpet for the silver chain that holds

Mama and Daddy's wedding rings and spot it shining from beneath the couch. But when I bend to reach it, I hear Powder's wild barking and Dante's yelp from the kitchen.

His magazine was too close to a lit burner and has erupted in flames. In a swift move, Dante grabs the faucet and aims it at the fire before anyone can stop him. And then a small mess erupts into a bigger one. We're all frozen in horror watching the flame roar up the backsplash on the wall until Bailey's scream jolts us back into the moment. Ari flies into the laundry room, and I rush forward to grab Bailey. I yell at Dante to follow, but he stands frozen until I find the strength to lift him into the living room with Miles. I run back into the kitchen, sweat pouring from my forehead, and follow Zion and Korey's lead, grabbing a towel and beating at the spreading blaze until Korey's rag catches fire too. Zion snatches it from him, throwing it in the sink just as the smoke detector goes off.

"Get the kids out," Zion shouts at me. I'm about to argue, thinking we can still stop this, but one look at the gathering black smoke is enough to make me obey. Just as I'm about to grab the front knob, Ari bursts through the laundry room door, rips the pin out of the red fire extinguisher, and white powder blasts toward the flames.

"Sorry," she squeaks when the flame is extinguished.

Zion and Korey got caught in the blast and are covered in the white powder, coughing up a storm. Ari rests the fire extinguisher on the table and moves to turn the stove fan on to disperse the smoke. My heart still feels like it's gonna beat out of my chest, but the relief that consumes me is palpable. The kitchen is a mess, but at least we still have a house. At least none of us got hurt.

Zion and I fan the smoke detector while Korey moves to open the window as the alarm continues to blare. But then I see Bailey jumping on the couch, pointing wildly at the door as Dante sobs on the floor.

Miles squeals excitedly, running toward it.

Ari runs behind him, yelling, "You're not allowed to answer the door!" But he gets to it first, twisting the handle and pulling it free just as she grabs him up in the air.

It's our social worker. The blond woman's briefcase drops to the ground, her expression transforming from concern to an almost-comedic look of shock as she takes in the scene. We all freeze. My towel lies limp where I was just fanning the air, balanced on a chair.

"Ms. Lusby," Ari says, adopting a professional tone, "if you'd just give us a moment, we'd be happy to welcome you in." Ari closes the door in the woman's face before slamming her back against it with a look of pure terror. "Surprise visit!" she whisper-yells, and finally, the smoke detector stops.

Ms. Lusby sits across from me in a green blouse and slacks with a serious expression on her face. The kitchen reeks of smoke, despite our open windows, and I know she's only doing her job, but I can't help but feel frustrated. If she'd shown up just five minutes earlier, she would've seen a picture-perfect family. This was supposed to be a routine surprise visit, but now she has to investigate what happened with the fire and "figure out if further action needs to be taken."

"Novah, I'm telling you the same thing I told each of your siblings. It's okay to be completely honest with me. I'm here to help, not hurt. I just want to make sure everyone's stories match up."

I exhale, resting my palms on the kitchen table. "And I already told you what happened, Ms. Lusby. My story's not gonna change, and I know for sure all of us are telling you the same thing. I mean absolutely no disrespect to your process, but when would Ari have had the time to coach any of us to lie? You literally knocked on the door while everything was happening."

"Just tell me one more time," Ms. Lusby says patiently, pen poised over her notebook.

"We were all sitting either here in the kitchen or in the living room doing homework and Korey was cooking. I'm telling you—it looked like we could've been in a breakfast commercial or somethin'. Dante came downstairs—"

"I thought you said you were all downstairs?"

"All of us but Dante. He's smart, even skipped a grade last year—remember? He finished his work before us, went upstairs to get a new dinosaur magazine, got distracted like ten-year-olds do, and accidentally put it too close to a burner.

"I got the kids out of the kitchen, Ari ran to get the fire extinguisher, and Zion and Korey and I tried to beat the flames down until Ari extinguished the fire. Everything literally happened in under two minutes."

"And do you all typically let Dante cook often?"

I scoff. "I'm sorry. It really feels like you're trying to trip me up! I said it was Korey cooking. And thirteen going on fourteen is more than old enough to use a stove responsibly."

We stare at each other, until she lets out a small exhale and scribbles something in her yellow notepad. I lean back, arms crossed over my chest, and glance over at the clock. My date's in an hour and a half, and it'll take at least forty-five minutes to get ready.

"Okay, Novah. I really do believe all of you, I just have got to be sure. You understand that in this profession, abuse or neglect is not always 'in your face,'" she says, doing air quotes. "I want the best for all of you."

I nod quickly. "No, I get it." I'm not trying to give her a hard time on purpose. It's just that this process is so irritating. How am I expected to be perfectly calm while she tries to determine whether any of us will still have a home with our family by the end of the hour?

"Good. So these are my last two questions, and they might be upsetting, so brace yourself."

I purse my lips, but nod again for her to continue.

"Do you feel safe here?"

"Yes. There's no place I'd rather be."

"Okay, and the last," she says, leaning forward with her hands clasped, and somehow the look in her eye makes the energy shift and I feel unprepared. "The custody hearing is set for early in the new year, and it seems to me that you're counting on your sister being granted full custody. But how do you honestly think Ariana's doing with you all? With everything? It's a high-pressure situation, don't you think?"

I immediately think of when I asked Korey a similar question after the Mrs. Lucas blowout. "Considering who she was before and who we all are now"—I shrug—"she's trying her best."

"And is her best enough?"

I hesitate for a moment. My instinct is to scream no. I want to tell someone how overwhelmed I am. For a second, I'd like to confide in her that the only thing I've thought of more than Hailee since last night is how much I wish I could really apply for that news internship. I want to tell her that I wish so many of my dreams hadn't died with my parents. Or how I didn't honestly have faith in those dreams even before they died. But that will only diminish her faith in Ari, so I don't say any of it.

"Her best is enough, because we're all doing this together," I say, looking her square in the eyes. "We all look out for one another. We all love one another. We all take care of one another. And if we have each other, Ms. Lusby—if we're allowed to stay together, we're gonna be okay."

◊◊◊

"Thank you so much for understanding, Ms. Lusby," Ari says, following her out the door so they can speak privately. What is usually an hour-long social worker home visit turned into a two-and-a-half-hour-long interview session—Ari's being the longest. But in the end and after Ms. Lusby called her supervisor, all our answers matched up. For a minute there, I wasn't so sure how things would swing. But I wanted to fall on my knees in thanks when Ari sent a discreet thumbs-up our way after her interview. We were convincingly happy, and the situation was deemed "entirely accidental." Which it was, but you never know exactly how these things will end, especially when your social worker has caught a conditional guardian and her six dependents in a smoky house when the ten-year-old is distraught, the seven-year-old and five-year-old are uncooperative, and two of the other children are covered in remnants of extinguishing powder.

"Well, that was a shit show," Ari says when she walks back in and sits across from me at the table. I rewrap the towel on my damp locs like a turban and watch as her forehead hits the table with a thump.

I bite my lip, wanting to make her feel better. She looked like she was about to pass out the entire time Ms. Lusby was here. The threat of failure is forever looming over us like a dark cloud ready to send a lightning bolt to strike with no notice.

I lean toward her in my chair. "My favorite part . . . was Korey excusing himself so he could get ready for Saturday detention on time."

A muffled chuckle and her bobbing shoulders let me know she's smiling. Ari sits up, not bothering to move the twists from her face.

"My favorite part was when Miles told her 'Spider-Man defeats villains who try to steal his family.'"

I stand, barking a laugh as I go to grab fruit for us from the fridge. Korey's powder-covered breakfast had to be discarded too.

Ari pops a piece of cantaloupe into her mouth and then fills up her bowl. "Where is everybody?"

"Miles went down for a nap, like, ten minutes ago, Zion's getting ready for work at Acosta's, and Bailey and Dante are watching TV in Mama and Daddy's room."

"Good," she sighs. "You wanna watch a movie? There's a Hunger Games marathon," Ari says, wiggling her brows. "I mean, I gotta go to the shop at four to talk to Antoinette about some money stuff after I go to the bank, but I can at least watch one movie."

I pick watermelon seeds out of a piece on my fork, avoiding her eye. Now's as good a time as any to ask. "Actually, I have a date in a couple minutes. Hey, do you think this is too casual?" I stand so she can fully see the burnt-orange wide-leg jumpsuit Oma, Kedijah, and Monae voted on last night.

"No, it's cute." Her voice perks up. "A date? Who's the lucky girl?"

"Hailee from the shop. She's really sweet. We're gonna meet at Houey's for shaved ice."

"Oh, that's a cute first date. Wait. The Houey's on Marlboro Pike? Isn't that kinda far?"

I shake my head. "It's only a twenty-minute drive, and I'd be back with the car by three so you can get to work."

Ari scoffs, her mouth hung open and big brown

eyes wide in disbelief. "I'm sorry, are you asking what I think you're asking?"

"It'll be really quick, Ari, please!"

"Novah, you have your learner's, not your license yet," she says seriously.

"So? Daddy always said I was the quickest learner out of the three of us when he was teaching me to drive at fifteen! And you've seen me drive. I'm always super careful."

She shakes her head, standing to grab a cranberry juice out of the fridge. "I only ever let you drive up the street. Ten, maybe twelve minutes max."

"This is just an extra ten minutes, and I promise I'll text you as soon as I get there!"

She scratches her forehead with her eyes closed, and I can see her decision written all over her face. "Look, we just got that SUV and it's our only way to get around right now. I don't have a choice here when you're uninsured."

I lean back in my chair with folded arms. "Why is it that whenever you need to get somewhere or wanna do something—"

But Ari waves her hands, exhaustion covering every inch of her face as she speaks over me. "No, Novah! Don't argue with me today, because I promise you, you're gonna lose. We just got over this social worker mess. We *fought a fire* this morning. I'm tired, and really, it was stupid for you to even ask. I'm sure Hailee's a great girl. And I'm not saying you can't go or catch a ride. Hell, Uber for all I care. But that car stays in the driveway until I or Zion puts the keys in the ignition, and that's final." She grabs her bowl from the table, heading for the stairs. "I'm gonna go take a nap with Miles. Enjoy your date, or don't? I'm too tired to care."

I watch her ascend the steps, seething as my foot taps erratically on the hardwood. She can hang out with her friends with the car. She can drive back and forth to work and wherever the hell else she chooses to go in the *family* car, but the rest of us have to sit around and wait and miss out?

A buzz in my pocket makes me jump, but it's just my phone. A text from Hailee.

> About to leave! Is 1:30 still good?

I rip the towel from my head, standing to lean on the counter, and then I see them—the keys—hanging on the ring, just calling out to me. But I pull up Uber and request a ride instead. Olivia in a Honda Civic will be arriving in three minutes.

> Yep, 1:30's great! Meet you there

I grab my small purse from the chair and slip my slides on, stomping across our creaky floor, but I pause when I see Ari's open wallet sitting on the small table in the walkway. I can't drive the car? Fine. But Ari is gonna finance my date today. I grab a couple bills, certain she won't miss the money anyways, and slip them into my bag.

CHAPTER 12

I reject Hailee's offer to pay, handing a bill to the cashier, and minutes later we walk away with two monster-sized shaved ices. Hailee's is a flavor mix of birthday cake, buttercream, and mango with gummy bears, Nerds, and whipped cream to top. I played it safe, ordering marshmallows and sour gummy worms to top my strawberry shortcake shaved ice.

"TikTok or YouTube?" Hailee asks, picking up our question game.

"Oh, TikTok, for sure," I say with no hesitation, and then ask, "Doja Cat or SZA? And remember, there *is* a correct answer."

"Oooh, that's a tough one." She wrinkles her nose. "Okay, lyrically, I'd have to go with Doja, but I definitely enjoy staring at SZA more. Actually," she says, looking at me with her head at a slight tilt and squinted eyes, "you kinda favor her with the fullness of your lips and shape of your mouth. You even have a beauty mark on your bottom lip."

I raise a hand to my chest. "SZA?! I— Hailee, don't

make me blush out here, okay? I honestly don't think there's a better compliment."

"Hey, it's the truth," she says matter-of-factly. I cheese, settling in at the round purple picnic table across from her and finally raising a scoop to my mouth, but Hailee's hands fly up, and she says, "Wait! I wanna document this moment!" She digs in her crossbody yellow satchel for her phone. "Ten years back my dad and I had *the best* authentic southern shaved ice in New Orleans, and then last year when he brought me here, I didn't believe him when he said this place was almost better. But. It. Is."

I pose for the camera first, holding the treat to my pursed lips, and then slip it in my mouth. And my brows fly up in surprise. The taste of the strawberry isn't overwhelmingly sweet, and there's a creamy texture that makes me scoop another helping before I can swallow the first.

Hailee nods. "See! I know what I'm talking about, huh?"

She grabs her cup and moves to sit beside me so I can see the pics.

"Oh, you gotta send that to me." I look like I've just experienced pure bliss, like I could be walking through the gates of heaven at any moment.

Hailee props her phone up against the bar holding the umbrella above us as we pose for three timed pictures. I expect her to step away after, but she stays next to me, our arms brushing as we continue eating.

I tell Hailee about this morning's fire incident, and she laughs so hard, we start drawing eyes from those sitting around us. I leave out the whole threat-of-separation-by-social-services thing, not wanting to ruin the mood.

She wipes a happy tear from her eye. "Oh my gosh. I swear Miles is my favorite, but Miss Bailey just has that smile that makes you feel like . . . I dunno. Like happiness lies within her or something. You got it too!"

I look away from her, suddenly shy, but the rise in my cheeks is a tell-all. "Well, if you ever wanna babysit. Please, tell me. You'll be worn out afterward, but it'll be a ball."

And she actually nods eagerly. "I'd love to, Nov! I've always wanted a little sibling, but it was always just me and my sister, Carmen. And she's ten years older. Then, after our mom passed, she really did take on the mother role instead of sister."

My eyes go wide. I'd known about her mother passing, but I hadn't realized that her big sister was the one actually raising her. Still, I'm careful not to dig too deep. Sometimes people bring up my parents in conversation and it feels natural, because once upon a time, they did walk this earth with us. They did live and breathe and strive and succeed. We *should* be able to talk about them. But other times, the mere mention of them makes my stomach go tight. It makes my throat close and my eyes burn. And occasionally—and this is my least favorite—my body will decide it's time to have a full-on panic attack.

I avoid asking direct questions about her mom and instead focus on the one really burning a hole through my tongue. "What was it like being raised by your sister?"

Hailee stares into her cup, scooping and dropping the ice over and over again. "Honestly, not horrible. Well, it was at first because all of a sudden it was like one of my best play partners and friends had to 'lay down the law' and be responsible for everything, including herself and me. And that made her . . . less fun . . . and annoying. But eventually I think the way I viewed her changed. I mean, she lost her mom too and then she jumped so willingly into the role. You can't not respect her, right? Even my dad wasn't ready for the responsibility, but my sister didn't hesitate." She pushes her cup away from her, wiping her mouth with a napkin as she stares ahead. "Maybe it's because I was so young at the time, but now when I hear the word *mom*, both my mom and Carmen come to mind. Like equally."

I nod, looking down at the bracelet Mama gave me.

That all sounded familiar. Ari didn't hesitate either. I suddenly feel the few remaining stolen bills in my pocket weighing me down like an anchor. I already knew I had enough money to pay for our shaved ice before I took money out of Ari's wallet. I was just so mad that she always gets her way . . . and now that that feeling's passed, guilt settles in.

"I'm really glad you guys were able to make it work," I say quietly.

"Me too. I didn't think we would at first." After a beat, she says, "Hey, can I ask you a question?" And when she looks up at me again, her eyes are full of sadness and I have to resist the urge to reach out and hug her like I would with one of my little siblings. "Do you ever feel with Ari like you being there is too much for her?"

I don't mean to laugh, but I do and then clamp my hand over my mouth when I see her expression. "I'm sorry," I rush. "It's just that yeah, I do feel like that all the time and it's wild that you just voiced it out loud. Sometimes I feel like if Ari just didn't have me to deal with, and only my other siblings, she'd be a lot happier . . . And maybe then everyone in the house would be too." My voice kind of falls off, and I can't believe I just said that out loud to Hailee. On our first date. And why had she asked? Has she been able to tell just how much Ari couldn't stand me the few times she'd seen us interact in school? And then she nods with understanding.

"I get that. I mean, it's just me at the house. But at the same time I feel like my dad acts like having to pause his life to raise me now is an inconvenience for him. Which is super annoying because this was his idea in the first place. Because I was fine where I was at," she says angrily, and her arms fly into the air in exasperation.

And then when she looks at me, embarrassed for her own outburst, I just smirk. "No, I get it."

We're quiet for a while as I finish my shaved ice and pop a gummy worm into my mouth and offer Hailee one. She takes it and does the same, offering a green gummy bear (my favorite), and then says, "Can I ask you a kind of personal question?"

"Oh god, another one," I laugh, shifting my locs out of my eyes.

"No, no, I promise this one is so much easier," she says, raising her hands, and I give her the go-ahead. "Have you ever been in a relationship before?"

I feel a surge of relief. A little question about my sad love life is nothing compared to talking about dead parents and siblings raising siblings.

"Oh, not one," I say with a shake of my head. "I mean, in eighth grade there was this girl, Tanisha, that I had a huge crush on. And the night of our winter formal, we danced and I had my first kiss under the shining stars the decorating committee stuck on the ceiling of the middle school gym—it was beautiful. Like the cute, romantic stuff you see in those coming-of-age movies, ya know? But she ended up moving to Vermont the next year and we lost touch. I won't even pretend like I wasn't devastated." I chuckle at how ridiculous it all sounds. But Hailee is looking at me like it's the most adorable little story she's ever heard. "What about you?" I ask. "I bet you left all those southern belles in full-blown tears when they found out you were moving up north."

Hailee laughs into her hands, shaking her head. "Not even close. My first girlfriend was really just a fling the summer before I left. She was a long-lost camp friend I thought I'd never see again, and when we reconnected, we were, like, *infatuated* with one another. She promised we'd make it work even though I was moving, but then my sister saw her making out with some girl on a bench in the middle of Lenox Mall for the world to see and sent me pictures of them in action."

"Oh no," I say. "That's brutal."

But Hailee waves her hand dismissively. "It's *super* fine," she says, laughing. "Even though I was devastated at first too. I'm pretty sure my dad wanted to send me back when I wouldn't stop blasting Olivia

Rodrigo and Taylor Swift songs for a week on repeat. But I got over it and the next thing I knew, I was accidentally calling you cute to your friend's face." She cringes slightly and closes her eyes, obviously still embarrassed. "I swear it just slipped out and I was like, Oma's nice, but the first thing she's gonna do is run and tell Novah what I said. Did she?"

"Oh yeah." I nod vigorously. "She told me the very moment she found me in the hall, and I mean, she ran straight from debate class with her book bag bopping on her back and was weaving through kids like it was an obstacle course." I clap my hands, laughing. "You shoulda seen it. She was bent over, out of breath, and the words came in between her inhaler pumps, but she got it out eventually."

Hailee drops her head into her hands and laughs with embarrassment.

"I was happy to hear it, Hailee. Thrilled, for real. Just too shy myself to say anything to you at the time, but . . ." I scoot closer to her and cross my legs, fumbling with my buzzing phone in my lap. "I think . . . you're pretty gorgeous yourself." The words come out slowly and definitely sound as scared as I am, but at least they're out. She drops her hands, smirking as she mouths a soundless thank-you.

And when her big eyes find mine, my filter shuts off even as butterflies flutter in my chest. "I'm really happy that you made the jump to ask me out because . . . I've liked you since last school year, and I don't think I ever would've gathered the courage to ask you myself."

Her warm hand rests on top of mine, and I flip it, interlacing our fingers. "I've liked you for a really long time too, Nov."

Reluctantly, I pull my eyes away, unable to ignore the relentless buzzing on my phone. My heart, which was soaring past the clouds a second ago, suddenly drops.

I have seven texts from Korey. He got in a fight with two kids in detention, and he's begging me to come get him from the nurse's office.

"I'm so sorry, Hailee," I say, fumbling with my phone, "I have to go."

CHAPTER 13

Vice Principal Brinkley's accolades hang on the wall behind the bald, angry man scowling at me and Korey. I'd hurried into his office ten minutes ago, and no matter what we say, he won't budge. He keeps looking down on Korey like he's some sort of problem child beyond saving, which makes me want to fling myself over the desk and hit him. But instead I hold an angry grip on the back of Korey's chair, listening as Vice Principal Brinkley proposes further punishment.

"I didn't start it," Korey insists. His words come mumbled through the ice bag he holds against his bottom swollen lip. Other than a cut on his brow and a pounding headache, he'll be fine. Much better than Hugh McFoy, who's sporting a black eye, and Justin Branson, whose nose may be broken. They're still with the nurse.

Vice Principal Brinkley's arms fly up in exasperation. "Mr. Wilkinson, what would you call throwing the first punch?"

"Defending myself! They tried to jump me!"

"Ms. Newsom said you threw the first *two* punches. One at Hugh, then one at Justin. If you ask me, then it sounds like the two kids who just got punched in the face are the ones actually defending themselves." The mustached man leans forward on the desk with stern eyes. "Now, you started the day with detention; it looks like a three-week suspension should follow."

I inhale sharply as fear settles over me. We were warned that detentions wouldn't look good on the record when the judge reviewed our case. But a three-week suspension is nothing short of disastrous—Ms. Lusby will be telling each of us to pack a bag by the end of the month. "No, no, no. Wait a second, Mr. Brinkley. You don't even have the full story here and you're ready to throw out suspensions?"

"I have the full story," he says, looking bored, and I feel my anger burning. How can he sound so nonchalant when this decision could lead to our family being ripped apart?

"Korey's been through a lot, and some boys, who were *also* in Saturday detention, getting in his face and calling him stupid doesn't sound innocent—and I mean, what kind of people even do that? Sounds like bullying to me. Isn't this one of those no-tolerance-for-bullying schools?"

His sharp eyes fly to me. "Yes, and Mr. McFoy and Mr. Branson will be dealt with, but we also have a no-tolerance rule for fighting. I should be expelling your brother—"

My heart skips a beat. "You can't—"

"And now that I think about it, you aren't Korey's legal guardian, and I shouldn't even be speaking to you about this matter. Where is your sister, Miss Wilkinson?"

"I'm right here," Ari says, flying into the office and taking a seat beside Korey. "I'm so sorry I'm late, Vice Principal Brinkley. I was at the bank when I got the call." Her eyes cut at me, and I shrink behind Korey from the severity in her glare. But why are her angry eyes directed at me? Because I showed up before she did? What? Is she going to yell at me again for "pretending" to be the one in charge?

"That's all well and fine," he says, nodding at her, "but we need to discuss your little brother, as he's proving that he's well on his way to becoming a promising delinquent. Now, I got the call from—"

"One second, Vice Principal Brinkley," Ari says, and pushes her keys into my hands. "I'm Korey's guardian, and I'm the only person that needs to be present in here right now. Novah, go sit with the kids in the car."

"But—" both Korey and I start, but one striking glance from Ari's bulging eyes silences us. Korey was right. Those are Daddy's eyes, and challenging her right now isn't worth it.

◇◇◇

I'm sitting in the car with Miles, Bailey, and Dante when Ari and Korey walk out of the school building thirty minutes later. I can tell from the wild motions of Ari's arms and Korey's downcast eyes that she's still berating him. But when I hop out of the driver's seat, I see her attention switch to me. I stand nervously with my arms crossed over my stomach and lean against the car. Maybe I should've called her after Korey called me, but I already knew the school was going to, so that would've been a waste of time. Korey's voice on the phone had sounded scared. And that's just not a common emotion he exhibits. Plus, I don't have to be a guardian to show up when our siblings need help. Ari knows that.

But as they get closer, I'm not seeing mere anger in her eyes. It feels like . . . fury? Nothing I could've done would warrant that look.

"When Korey called, I—"

"The money," she demands, holding out a hand.

My face burns. In the confusion of the day, I'd completely forgotten about the money I took from Ari earlier.

I dig in my purse, saying, "I'm so sorry," but she slashes a *zip it* sign in the air, and I do.

Without taking her eyes off my face, she says,

"Korey, in the car. Dante, close the doors and roll up the window."

Neither of them dares argue as I remove the small bundle of bills and hold them out.

But Ari paces back and forth before landing in front of me with her hands on her hips and an eerily calm tone. "Okay. I need to understand. What was your thought process?"

"I was just mad that you wouldn't let me take the car for my date, so I slipped a couple bills out of your purse, but I never even thought you'd notice. And I planned to replace it," I blurt out, even though the thought of replacing the money hadn't actually occurred to me until this very moment.

"You didn't think I'd notice," she screams suddenly. "Novah, I told you I was going to the bank today. How could you not care that we'd be over three hundred dollars short for Lively's rent payment? How do you just decide that your feelings are a priority over your family's livelihood?"

My mouth drops open. "Three hundred dollars?!" I stammer. "I only took—" But my words fail as my eyes fall to the bills I'm holding in my hands. I thought I'd taken a small stack of folded five- and one-dollar bills. Hell, Hailee's and my shaved ice didn't even amount to ten dollars. But when I use a finger to peel back the two fives, there are three crisp

one-hundred-dollar bills staring back at me. My eyes
fly from the bills between us to Ari's furious expression. Who folds hundred-dollar bills into fives and
ones?!!

"Ohmygod, I swear I thought those were small
bills."

But her face is a mask of disbelief as she reaches out
and snatches the money from my hand. "Yeah right!"
she scoffs.

"Ari, I swear! I would never take that much money
when I know it goes to the mortgage and the rent or
food and clothes. You have to believe that."

"Oh, do I? I'm supposed to believe you wouldn't
steal money. When you just admitted to it."

"I only admitted to taking, like, twenty dollars!"

"Yeah right, you little klepto! Are you ready to
admit that it was you stealing all that money from the
register for the past month too?" she says, getting in
my face with her arms crossed over her chest.

It feels like my brain is short-circuiting. Taking
money from the register has never even crossed my
mind. How could she think I'd do that? Why would
she think I'd put our family in danger like that? I
would never jeopardize the outcome of our custody
over some petty argument. "Ari, I have never touched
money from the register," I say, keeping my voice level,
pleading for her to believe me.

Her hands run through her twists in frustration, and then she's pacing again, but with a finger up to keep me silent. And then the laugh that escapes her lips seals the deal, and I know for sure she doesn't believe me before her mouth even opens. "I never thought of you as a liar. And I really wouldn't expect you to steal from your family. But I think what I'm struggling with the most is how selfish you really are."

That comment flips a switch and outrage consumes me. "Selfish? Me!" I say, jabbing at my chest. "What world are we living in where you have the right to ever call me selfish! I pick up the kids from school. I never miss shifts at work. I help out with homework, bath times, and bedtimes more than you and Zion ever have. When my friends ask me to go out, I say no because I know I have responsibilities. Even if you don't!"

Ari takes a step toward me, and instinctively I step back, but I can't stop the angry words from leaking out of my mouth. "I fall asleep in class and miss assignments because I'm so exhausted from running around and doing everything for everyone except for myself, including covering for you."

"And then you go and compensate yourself by stealing money from my purse and the cash register and think I'm too stupid to see hundreds of dollars going missing."

I hear a door open and close behind me, but my eyes are stuck on Ari's face.

"What? You really thought you could steal all that money but as long as you ran around trying to be better than me that I wouldn't care?" Ari says, crossing her arms over her chest. "Is that why you came here and swooped in to try and play the hero? To try and outdo me, and then I wouldn't care that you're a thief?"

"I came here because Korey called me because he trusts that I'll always come through to help him. I'm guessing he didn't call you for that same reason."

She flinches, but then her shock dissolves and her eyes narrow. "And when I walked in, he was facing a three-week suspension. Is that how you help?" Bailey walks over and pulls the tail end of Ari's tank top for her attention, but she's too caught up in yelling in my face to notice.

"Like you could've done so much better!"

"I did! He only has to do three days of in-school suspension now because of me. Because I talked Vice Principal Brinkley down. And this will be a whole lot easier to explain to our social worker than a three-week suspension. Don't you think?"

"I—"

"How could you do this, Novah? And on the day where we already had to talk Ms. Lusby out of trying to remove all of you from our home?" she continues, her eyes welling up. "Today you do this? Today you steal and then have the audacity to act insulted for getting caught and attack my decisions? You really think today, of all days, is the one that you have a right to criticize my parenting?"

Bailey taps Ari relentlessly, and when she raises her hands to sign, Ari steps back, yelling, "No, Bailey! If you want to say something, then say it! I hear you with Miles, okay! We all know you can still talk!"

Bailey's tears are immediate and so is Ari's remorse. Her hands fly to her mouth, horrified.

But I snatch Bailey up as she cries into my neck. "That was over the line," I spit. "You know her therapist said not to." Ari motions toward us, and I step out of her reach.

"You really still think you're doing a great job with us? Because lately I've been wondering if you stepped up because it was the right thing to do, or if it's so we can all fall at your feet and give you the praise you think you deserve for keeping your *siblings* out of foster care, Ari! And how could you, considering what a piss-poor job you're doing! Since Mama and Daddy died, this family's been falling apart, and you're barely even around enough to notice!"

When she doesn't say anything, I just shake my head, holding Bailey even closer. "Look, the fake nice thing obviously isn't working for us, okay? I'll keep on doing everything for the kids and you and everybody but myself, and you keep on showing up to work and home late and putting yourself first. We both know there's only one person selfish between us, and it's you. You can add cruel to that now too."

"Bai, I'm so sorry," Ari says through her fingers.

I throw the keys at her, turning to walk away. A mix of Bailey's tears and snot streams down my chest as her sobs quicken. And when I hear Ari's voice again, I can tell she's crying too. "I— Novah, where are you going?"

"To the house," I say, not bothering to look back. "We'll walk."

CHAPTER 14

I'm daydreaming in the back of my World History class when a flash of movement catches my eye. When I turn, I see Hailee smiling broadly on the other side of the closed door as she gestures at her phone.

"Eyes on your own test, Wilkinson," Mr. Lane says, and my eyes snap forward.

I return my focus to my test paper, but no amount of focus is gonna make the correct answers magically appear to me. But I pick up my pen, pretending to scribble out answers like Monae is actually doing two desks to my right.

Last night I was far too busy giving Ari the silent treatment to accept Monae's offer to study together. But as I add up all these short answer points I'm missing, I realize that my pettiness may not have been as worth it as I thought.

It was the first time in a long time that both Zion and Ari were home to help with the kids and the house. I don't know what was up with Zion, but Ari finally stopped asking me to cover for her. Really, she's stopped asking me to do anything. We haven't spoken in almost two weeks—since our blowout at the school. Bailey may be quick to forgive, but I'm not that easy.

My phone buzzes in my jacket pocket, and discreetly, I slide it out.

> **Hailee:** My last period let out early so I'm headed to Lively's. You sure it's fine for me to use that spare locker?

> **Novah:** It's no problem at all 👍

I press send, smiling to myself. It's immature to give Hailee Ari's spare locker, but I just knew it would irritate her, and that made it worth it. Why should Ari get two lockers when the rest of us have one? Why did she think it was okay to rule with an iron fist and why did she think we'd all follow her blindly when she didn't deserve it? I'm sick of it, and Ari is gonna learn one way or another to start picking up her own slack.

"All right, that's the time, class," Mr. Lane says as the last bell rings. "Pass your test forward and have a good weekend. Oh, and Ms. Wilkinson," he says just as I'm tossing my bag onto my shoulder, "I'd like to speak to you for a moment."

I make no move to hide my irritation, letting my

head fall in annoyance as I slide into a desk at the front of the room, but Mr. Lane doesn't seem to care. He moves around his desk, leaning on it with crossed legs as the last student exits the room.

"We've been talking about this test for the last two weeks," he starts. "It wasn't some huge surprise. So please, explain to me why you were so unprepared?"

I grimace. "You haven't graded the test yet. How would you already know I was unprepared?"

He considers that for a second, and then my stomach drops when he turns to search through the stack, finding my test in record time. He flips through the pages and then turns it for me to see.

All the smiley faces and little suns and houses I'd doodled over the blank page stare back at me.

"I'm getting entirely too familiar with your bad artwork in my history class, okay? I get that the last couple of months have been . . . difficult for you. But I have been more than accommodating. I give you extra time on assignments that are still somehow late and offer you extra credit that never sees my in-box. Ariana would never come into my class as unprepared as you do."

"I'm not Ariana."

"Even your brother, who was clearly uninterested in the subject, never showed your obvious lack of commitment to his academics. They both had dreams and goals that they were working toward, and I gotta be honest, I don't see any of that in you."

My head snaps up from my bracelet, and I stare at Mr. Lane with as much disdain as I can muster. I have dreams and I have goals. Just because they feel unattainable doesn't mean they don't exist. And putting everything else that actually matters before caring about his stupid class doesn't make that a lie.

"Mr. Lane, I didn't have time to study for your test because I've been busy with my family and work," I say dully, adjusting my book bag as I stand. "Because I have a job that I actually need to be at right now."

As I turn to walk away, he says, "And what about your essay on the last ice age or the two-page paper you were supposed to hand in on Monday about the Neolithic Revolution? Huh?"

I reluctantly turn back to him. I was almost done with the paper, but I'd completely forgotten about the essay he gave me an extension on last week. An extension I begged for. I hate that he's right, because World History is not a class I can afford to fail. It isn't even hard—just a nuisance. But I don't want this silly class to be something that could be used against us at the hearing in January. "Right, right," I say slowly. "I will be sure to get you both of those by Monday. I promise."

He shakes his head with a sad laugh. "And I'm sorry to say it, but at this point, Wilkinson, your promises mean nothing to me. I mean, I don't know what I need to do to even motivate you. Or make you pretend like you care. Were you telling the truth when you said you had to help your sister with her speech lessons, or was that just an excuse to get out of last week's monotheism assignment?"

"I wouldn't—"

"And skipping out on the one-on-one study session I offered to help you because you claimed you were short-staffed, but when I came in the shop later that day, things seemed to be running smoothly."

My mouth drops open in disbelief. "That's because I showed up!"

"Do I need to call Ariana and tell her how you've been slacking off? Would that make you care?"

I laugh to myself, shaking my head. That is the very last thing I need. Someone calling Ari to tell her I've been doing exactly what I accused her of—slacking off. I can already see the glee in her eyes at his words. But I don't care to let him know how much that call would bother me. "Call Ari if you want to, Mr. Lane. She was your fave, right?"

"Watch your tone," he snaps, holding a finger in my face with a stern expression.

But I throw my arms up in defeat, sighing, "I really am trying, Mr. Lane. I don't know what you want from me."

He turns, rounding the desk again, and begins straightening the test papers. "Wilkinson, I don't want to hear any more of your excuses. I don't want you turning in any more assignments late. And I want you to do better and at least try and make your sister proud if you don't care enough to do it for yourself."

My head tilts as I survey him through a squint. I am sick of being called a liar by him and the very person he is asking me to make proud. "I gotta be honest with you, Mr. Lane. Ariana's the last person I'm trying to impress right now."

Mr. Lane shrugs and grabs the eraser from a tray, saying, "Then show some initiative, take your work seriously, and try and make your parents proud," before turning to the board.

It's like I'm hearing every word he says following that from underwater. At first, I expect for the hives to come. I think the breath will be stolen from my lungs and my sight will blur. My vision does go, but that's because I see red and don't know what I'll do next. My immediate thought is to lob the four-hundred-page textbook I'm holding at his head, but the tiger's-eye crystal finds my sight line before the book can leave my hand. I feel a sob forming as Mama's face comes to mind, telling me to put it down. So I drop it and run out, ignoring Mr. Lane's demands behind me.

CHAPTER 15

When I knocked on Antoinette's door, she took one look at my pathetic puppy-dog eyes, shook her head with a pitying glance, and stepped to the side. I hadn't dropped in on her since last spring, when I used to just need a place to escape to. But today I couldn't take the silence of our house. Everyone was off at Lively's, where I was supposed to be too, but I couldn't bring myself to spend the whole day in Ari's presence, and quite frankly I missed Antoinette's apartment.

Almost every inch of the walls in the two-bedroom is covered in beautiful canvases or framed pictures of her friends and family. There's always the heavenly scent of spices from whatever new dish she's cooking on the stove, and best of all there isn't that overcrowded feel that takes over our house even when I am the only one home. Everything here could only belong to one of two people, and every single item has a place.

"One of you has got to bend eventually," Antoinette says after I update her on the Ari situation. She listened while bustling about her brightly decorated living room, straightening pillows and dusting lamps.

I lie sprawled across her emerald-green love seat, popping purple grapes into my mouth. "Well, it's not gonna be me, but when she's ready to apologize, I might consider listening."

"Funny," she says, walking by to knock my feet off her couch. "Ari said the same thing almost verbatim when she came to me crying and whining just like you are right now. You two are more alike than you think."

I pop up in the sofa, indignant. "I am not whining and crying."

"You are," she says, walking into the kitchen and adjusting the heat on the stove. "You're whining and crying and being childish because you know you were wrong about stealing that money"—she raises her voice, cutting me off before I can interrupt her—"even if you didn't mean to take as much as you did, Novah."

"I already apologized for that and she didn't believe me anyways. And what about her! You should've seen the way she acted, screaming in that public parking lot, calling me a klepto, *and* she was horrible to Bailey."

"And Ari sincerely apologized to Bailey and she accepted her apology. You know your sister was just lashing out because you took her outta her character and Bailey got caught in the crossfire. Now you wanna keep using that baby as an excuse not to woman up and speak to her? It's been three weeks, Novah!" She lets the wooden spoon rest in the pan, placing her hands on the counter and squinting at me. "And what are you even doing here? I saw your name on the schedule *you* made."

"I just—I'm here to do my homework. I have a lot to catch up on."

Antoinette glances from me to the brown book bag I dropped by the door with all my untouched books.

"No. You're really just here trying to punish her, huh? Yeah, I got sisters. I know what's up. You didn't show up and left her understaffed on purpose. Didn't you? Sounds to me like Ari might've been at least a little bit right about that selfish thing."

"It's more like she's finally getting a taste of her own medicine," I mutter, falling back in the seat. I don't even know why I came over here anymore. All Antoinette ever does is throw reason in my face. I'd forgotten.

"And you know what? I'd probably just leave you alone if you had actually come over here to do some schoolwork. Because I hear through the grapevine that you've been letting your grades slip."

"Antoinette, hearing something directly from Ari doesn't count as a grapevine, and I just needed someone to talk about everything with. Zion's never home, and he's always missing shifts, so I can't talk to him. Korey said everything you said, but meaner. Even Hailee said I may have done too much this time."

"And what about your friends?"

I shrug. "I haven't really brought it up with them yet."

She moves to sit next to me, bumping my shoulder. "So why aren't you with them talking about it now?"

"I dunno," I sigh, looking away from her. "Lately all the stuff I was desperate to do with them before just feels . . . less important. I don't care if I can't hang out at the mall or go to a late movie or to an escape room. I mean, it would be nice, but the kids always need help with something or have an appointment to be at, and then there's work—"

"Which you skip out on more and more to just sit around by yourself. I know those girls wanna be with you and help you, if you let them. Being on go all the time isn't cute, and girl, you are not a single parent."

I roll my eyes at her.

"If you need more help with the kids or time for yourself, then open your mouth and ask Ari."

"How am I supposed to do that when she's sneaking around and coming home late after hanging out with friends?"

Antoinette leans away, gazing at me with a squint. "You keep saying it, but do you really believe that, Novah? What friends is she hanging with? Almost all of them went on to different colleges with volleyball scholarships."

I stare at her, confused. That's a good point, but if she isn't with friends, then what is she doing? "What? Does she have a secret boyfriend or something?"

"What she has is . . ." Antoinette closes her mouth, seeming to change her mind about something mid-sentence. "What Ariana has is a lot on her plate. There are things that she does for herself to better herself and keep herself sane. You need to find something like that too. Something that doesn't involve accidentally steal-ing large sums of money or making your sister feel like trash for every horrible thing that's happened to you guys since the accident. That was unfair and you know it."

I look away from Antoinette, but she touches a soft finger to my chin. "Novah, call your friends, take a chance on that internship, and give Ari a chance to get the hang of things. Give yourself a chance too. You are still a kid, after all, I don't care what you think. Hell, all of you are. This is a serious real-life case of babies raising babies, and you all need each other even if some people are being too bullheaded to notice."

"Fine," I say, sitting up. "I'll think about it, but you believe me when I say I didn't touch that register money, right?"

"Hell yeah. You're a lot of things, but stupid isn't

one of them, and I know you wouldn't do that. Ari doesn't really believe it either anymore."

Keys jingle in the front door, and then it creaks open to reveal Omari, Antoinette's nineteen-year-old brother. When he was a kid, he played on the baseball team Daddy coached. Now, after dropping out of Towson, he works at Six Flags part-time and trades stocks.

My greeting gets lost in the air when Zion follows in behind him. I can tell just how much he didn't expect me to be sitting on the couch with the drop of his face.

"You're supposed to be at the shop," he says.

"And you said you were going in to work your shift at Acosta's."

Omari snickers, dapping me and bending to kiss his sister's cheek on the way to his room.

"Looks like we got two liars in the room now," Antoinette chuckles, walking into the kitchen to stir her pot. "Go ahead and confront each other. I'll try not to hear every word."

With that she taps her phone and a true crime podcast begins to play from the speakers.

Zion nods toward the door and I follow him out.

"Ari called asking about you," he says, closing the door behind me. "What are you doing here?"

I shake my head, not ready to admit the whole "trying to punish Ari" thing. It sounded a lot less clever after having Antoinette throw my childishness in my face. "I just needed a break and I didn't wanna be home alone."

"So why didn't you just tell her that?"

"Why don't you tell me why you're wandering in here smelling like weed and gearing up to play video games with Omari when you're supposed to be at work? Is this what you're doing when you miss all of our family dinners and shifts?"

Zion looks away from me, leaning on the railing to the first floor. He shakes his head too, exhaling deeply. "I haven't worked at Acosta's since the last week of August."

I can't do anything but blink at him as endless questions run through my mind. All this time, I've been going easy on him, because at least I knew he was actually working. I just assumed during most of those missed dinners or bath times that he was pulling overtime—that Mr. Acosta was really working him. But if he wasn't working at the grocery store, then he could've been home helping me. At least if Zion had been home, then I could actually stop pretending that I didn't want to apply for the news internship. My head cocks back as he avoids my eyes. "How, Zi? You literally come home in your green shirt every day."

"Yeah, well. They forgot to take one from me, so I put it on before I walk in the house."

I shake my head, still in disbelief. "But all of our groceries still come from there. I was just there last week and he let me use your thirty percent discount with no problem. Why would you quit?"

"Mr. Acosta really liked Mama and Daddy. So he let me keep the discount even after he fired me."

My inhale is sharp. "He *what*?! Why would he do that? Mr. Acosta is the nicest old man I've ever met."

"Turns out if you mess up enough inventory checks, daydream when you're supposed to be stocking shelves, and miss enough shifts, even the nicest old man any of us has ever met will still fire you."

He hops on the railing nonchalantly, and I resist the urge to push him as a sudden burst of anger rises in my chest. I've been blaming everything on Ari, mostly because she deserves it, but now that I think about it, when it comes to the kids, the only person around more than me has been Ari, not Zion. And now it turns out his absences weren't excusable? Maybe Ari shouldn't have been the only one receiving the full brunt of my annoyance. But when his eyes meet mine, I realize I'd read his body language wrong. That wasn't nonchalance. His eyes are guilt-ridden.

I exhale deeply, planting myself in front of him. "I don't get it, Zi. If you haven't been at work, where have you been? I dunno how you haven't noticed, but we've needed more help lately at home and at the shop." My voice softens. "And the kids miss you."

"I know, Nov, I'm sorry. But I didn't wanna disappoint Ari and tell her I'd need more money to make up for the cost of groceries since I lost my job, and then Bailey needed new shoes and Korey needed the entry money to enter that cooking contest next month too. I told her I could handle it all."

"But you couldn't."

"Wrong again. I could and I did. I've been doing little odd jobs around the neighborhood, you know— mowing lawns, fixing phone screens, tutoring for English. But I had to stop skimming money out the register when Ari started to notice."

My mouth drops open, and this time I want to strangle him. He hops off the railing, reading my thoughts, and takes a few quick steps back out of my reach. "Are you *kidding* me! She blamed me for that!" I hear blinds ruffle behind us and look back to see Antoinette's old neighbor shamelessly staring at us.

Zion holds his hands up in front of himself in defense. "Yeah, I know! Korey told me and I felt horrible, but I just— Novah, have you seen her eyes when she's pissed?"

"I did when she turned them on me three weeks ago, Zi!"

"I'm so sorry," he pleads, holding clasped hands out. "But I promise, it's all good now. I got a new part-time working the basketball station at Six Flags, since I only do half days at school this year. That's why I was with Omari. And I'm still doing work around the neighborhood too, so things should be more stable now—we can try and rebuild our cushion, and if we fall short on rent again, I'll be able to help get us where we need to be. I shouldn't have to miss any more shifts without notice, and I can help with the kids more, but you gotta promise you won't tell Ari it was me yet."

I scoff, but I already know I won't sell him out no matter how much he deserves it.

"Oh, and I'll be able to put the money I took back next week, so don't worry about it. And when I do, then I'll tell her. I swear."

I nod and then find myself chuckling at the relief on his face as we lean on the rail side by side. "You know, this whole time, I figured when you weren't at work or home, you might just be out here stalking Isabella."

"Nah. If Chris wants her, he can have her."

"All right, Zi. I won't tell her until you do. But you don't miss any more of our family dinners. That's the deal." I hold out my hand.

His brows knit. "Dante said you don't even speak to Ari at dinner. What do you care?"

"Hey, I have the leverage right now. Not you. Truth is, maybe the kids aren't the only ones who miss you."

His eyes brighten, and I see he's about to tease me

when he bites his lip, but I don't give him the chance, dramatically whipping my arm around with my hand out again. "Take the deal, because this is the last time Imma offer it."

He takes my hand, shaking it firmly, and then pulls me into a hug, lifting me off my feet.

CHAPTER 16

Zion lifts Miles out of the back seat of the Uber as Bailey, Dante, and I wait on the sidewalk outside the brick community rec building. This was supposed to be one of our family outings, finally with the whole family, to Korey's cooking competition. But Ari came up with some lame excuse and backed out last minute. With the "family car," of course. I try to shake away my attitude as we bustle into the gym now holding three makeshift cooking areas, but it's tough. Once again, Ari is finding time for herself and bailing on us when she knows how important this is to Korey.

We find seats high in the stands, waving at Korey in his custom blue apron and chef hat, just as the host, Rad Njenka, begins introducing the judges. A small camera crew for Channel 4 News pans the crowd before landing on the contestants.

"There will be just one round in the race to win the acclaimed City Teen Burger Competition," says Mr. Njenka from the court floor. "The winner will receive a chance to shadow the owner of the five-star

DC restaurant Urge for a day, earn a full scholarship to the Rochester Culinary Camp in New York this summer, and take home the fifteen-hundred-dollar prize money!" The crowd roars, and I snap a picture of Korey, looking unusually nervous at his station. When it comes to his cooking, he typically has an unshakable air of confidence, but this is his first official competition.

"You got this, Kor," Zion says, jumping up in his seat as the bell rings signaling the start of the first round. Korey begins rushing around the kitchen prepping ingredients for his cheesy breakfast burger. I stand, joining Zion in applause, and Dante, Bailey, and Miles hold up the colorful KOREY'S A WINNER sign they spent all morning crafting. Our hollering and hooting brings the camera crew and a woman with braids wrapped in a neat bun and a microphone our way. She speaks to the camera with her back to us, but I'm buzzing with excitement. I'd recognize Trinity Dawson anywhere.

"You should go talk to her later," a voice says from behind. I jump and turn to see Kedijah in the row behind us, smiling with her own little handmade GO KOREY sign. I mentioned the competition to her when we were texting last night—my attempt at taking Antoinette's advice.

"You came!" I step into her row, bear-hugging her before we sit. "I don't think so," I say, suddenly taking on some of Korey's nerves myself. "What would I say?"

"Just that you're a fan of her work! It doesn't have to be a job interview," she laughs. "But you literally watch her every day, and you've been following her on Twitter for, what? Two years. How could you not say hi?"

I bite the inside of my cheek and consider walking up to her, but what could I actually say that would hold her interest? I shake my head. "I don't wanna bother her. And she's working; wouldn't that be rude?"

"Nope," Zion says, turning in his seat, "but if someone's not afraid to be rude, it's definitely you." Bailey climbs out of Zion's lap and into Kedijah's, signing a mile a minute about acing her spelling test in school and the new doll Zion bought her yesterday. Kedijah's not fluent in ASL, so I'm saved from answering any further Trinity questions while interpreting.

◊◊◊

Forty-five minutes later, I'm leaning on the bathroom sink, scrolling my TikTok feed as Bailey hums in the stall. "Remember, we wipe front to back, Bai."

A toilet flushes in another stall, and when the door flies open, I try to disguise my gasp with a cough into my elbow.

"Great advice," Trinity says, heading to the sink and pumping the soap dispenser.

I give her a closed-mouth grin, unable to come up with any intelligent words.

She peers into the mirror at me with a squint, saying, "You look really familiar. Do we know each other?" Her airy tone contrasts her usual anchor voice.

"Uh, n-no," I stutter, and my voice has never been so high. "But I heard you may have known my dad. He owned Lively Pups. It's a dog-grooming shop."

She winces as she grabs a paper towel. I can tell just what she's remembering from the sad shift in her eyes. "I was so sorry to hear about your parents. They were such a sweet couple."

Luckily, her eyes don't stay sad for long. "I do remember twin little girls running around the shop the last time I was there. Are you . . . ?"

"Novah," I fill in, taking her outstretched hand. "And not twins. I'm a couple years younger than my sister Ariana."

"Right, right, Ariana. That's who the email address belonged to for your application?"

Application? My head cocks to the side in confusion. I never even allowed myself to open the application attached to the email Kedijah forwarded. "I'm sorry?"

"You know, you had the nicest little friend at that

career fair my boss forced me to go to. We had a great conversation that made the night worth it. She told me about you and your aspirations, so when I gave her my info, I thought I'd hear from you a lot sooner, but I'm thrilled you got your internship application in before the deadline on Monday."

The toilet flushes again, and Bailey pops out, still humming as she approaches the sink, waving at Trinity. She raises her arms, and I lift her so she can reach the soap and faucet while I balance her on one knee. "I'm sorry," I repeat, and my voice is shakier than I'd like. "Internship application?"

"Yeah, I was given your file with about six or seven applicants. But don't look so worried. I'm gonna make sure to put in a good word for you."

I set Bailey down, and she grabs five paper towels, jumping when a loud knock sounds at the door.

"They need you on the floor," says a deep voice from the other side.

"Hope to see you again," she says, nodding toward me and then bending at the knees. "And what's your name?"

Bailey signs it, and I'm ready to interpret, but Trinity's hands move quickly as she introduces herself and compliments Bailey's hair. Bailey beams, signing, "Novah likes watching you every day on the news. Over and over." And I chuckle, embarrassed.

Another set of knocking and Trinity heads toward the door, but I can't help but to ask, "Who was it again you said the email was from?"

"Your sister Ariana," she says, and walks out the door.

We walk into the hallway and stop at the water fountain so Bailey can refill her bottle. I pull out my phone to question Ari. I don't know what her intentions were in sending in that application, but it makes one thing clear for sure—she thinks she knows what's best for everybody and everything, and her complete disregard for this one single ask makes me want to rip every loc out of my scalp one by one.

It's not that I don't want this opportunity, anybody can see that I do. But I don't want to be a finalist only for the opportunity to be snatched away when I can't follow through.

Like when I tried out for track in eighth grade. The coach said he saw potential and Daddy said he'd be at tryouts, but then there was a mishap at the shop and he couldn't make it. I completely understood, but that night, when Ari asked him to be at her game, he said there was "nothing in the world" that could stop him from being there. Nothing. After that, going to the first practice just didn't feel important anymore.

It wasn't some dramatic, life-ending situation, but it did open my eyes. By the time track came around,

I'd tried dance, basketball, chess, and softball and followed through with none. Sometimes because I didn't want to, but more often because Zion was winning some writing competition, Bailey needed one-on-one time, Dante was a little genius, or one of my other siblings was doing something that needed Mama and Daddy's attention more.

Now Mama and Daddy aren't here anymore to give any of us attention. That's up to me, and Zion and Ari. Except I don't know where Ari is half the time and I'm sure Zion will be off next year to some four-year college. I don't want Korey, Dante, Bailey, or Miles to ever feel too lost in the confusion of our big family, even unintentionally. I don't want them to ever get to the point where they feel like their dreams are so unattainable that they're insignificant, because feeling grounded made dreaming hurt.

I delete my text and stuff my phone into my pocket. Ari doesn't listen to me anyways. Sending the text would just be like talking to a brick wall. Bailey tugs my shirt, asking to leave, and I hear applause and shouts coming from the auditorium. I pick Bailey up and run in just as Korey and a kid named Jess stand on either side of Mr. Njenka on the stage. The judges have deliberated and the third kid's already been eliminated.

"They called Louisa's garlic pizza burger dry and 'off-tasting,'" Dante says when we reach them in the stands. Miles sits on Zion's shoulders, using his head as a drum as one of the judges in a green dress hands Mr. Njenka an envelope.

"All right, folks," he says, staring around the room to add suspense. "After careful deliberation, the judges have come to a decision between Jess Hunnings's quesadilla burger with those exquisitely crisp tortilla buns or Korey Wilkinson's cheesy breakfast burger with a gooey egg cooked perfectly into that juicy patty." I smile with pride at that glowing review. Korey always said Salinger's made the best burgers, but the rest of us always agreed that his were better.

Mr. Njenka opens the envelope, playfully holding the card to his face as he looks from side to side. "Folks, the winner of this year's City Teen Burger Competition and fifteen-hundred-dollar prize money is . . ." The crowd holds a collective breath. ". . . KOREY WILKINSON!"

The auditorium explodes in screams and applause as Korey's eyes fly open—his arms raised in victory as a golden trophy is pushed into his hands.

I fly down the steps, toting Bailey, with my siblings on my heels as we run onstage, bombarding Korey with hugs. As we pose for a picture for the cameraman, I'm filled with joy seeing the look on Korey's face. Mama and Daddy wouldn't have missed this. And Ari shouldn't have.

CHAPTER 17

"Are you sure it's okay for us to drive to Six Flags?" Dante asks, hopping on my bed, watching me as I pack. I stuff a spare pair of pants and a Thor shirt into Miles's green backpack. Noise-canceling earphones and a pink visor in Bailey's unicorn bag. And water bottles wrapped in towels deep in my own. I have no plans to pay ten dollars for a drink today.

"Yes, it's not a problem, D," I say, avoiding his eyes. "You were there when I asked yesterday morning, right? Ari said it was fine for the four of us to spend the day at Six Flags, and she even gave us some spending money so we can get funnel cakes, Dippin' Dots, and a turkey leg. Isn't that your favorite?"

Miles starts bouncing at the mention of funnel cake as he slips his arms through the straps of his bag. He's overwhelmingly cute in his blue dinosaur shirt and a matching bucket hat.

"But you guys still aren't really even talking, because you stole a bunch of money," Dante says, following me around the room as I get myself ready, slipping on my sneakers. "Isn't she gonna be mad?"

"First of all, I didn't steal a bunch of money. That was just a misunderstanding. And no, she won't be mad, because I got my license last week, remember?"

"Provisional license."

I side-eye him. With my provisional, the law allows me to drive with my siblings in the car. The only problem is that I'm not on the insurance yet. But I will be soon, and we aren't going far. This is fine, and as long as everything goes to plan, I'll have the car back before Ari ever knows we were gone. "Yes, my provisional license, Dante. Look, you don't have to worry. Ari left yesterday to spend the night with some old friend at Howard. She's having fun and we get to too. And we do talk."

"Nuh-uh."

"Uh-huh! Now, can you go make sure Bailey is out of her bathing suit? It's October and the water park's not open."

Miles looks around the room like something's gonna pop out at us. "Where's Zi?"

"He works at Six Flags now, so we'll see him in a little bit when we get there." I throw my bag onto my shoulder, grab Bailey's, and he follows me out of the room and into the kitchen.

Ari *did* think it was a great idea for me to take the

kids up to Six Flags for the day. She even threw extra money at me so I'd stop asking questions about her little trip. Omari works security, so he can get us in free, and we'll be able to use Zion's discount on anything we'd need to buy. The only hitch is, yes, I told her we'd Uber there. But taking the car just makes sense. I hadn't been planning to when I asked Ari about taking the kids to Six Flags, but then she had a friend pick her up last night, Korey left to play basketball at the rec center, Zion caught a ride from Omari, and the car's just sitting in the driveway unused. It's a simple plan of convenience. Even better, Hailee's free (because I purposely didn't put her on the schedule), so she'll be able to meet us at the park by midday too. We talk every day now, but that's only at school, work, or over the phone. Today we'll finally get a chance to hang out without our responsibilities being the priority.

As long as we get back with the car before Ari, we're looking at what could be a perfect day, and that's a rare occurrence. She gets back at six, and I don't even want to think about her pulling up and seeing the car missing.

Bailey bounds down the steps in gray boots, a floral long-sleeve dress with just a sliver of her rainbow bikini strap peeking out, and a snooty look.

"Fine. Wear the bathing suit if you want, but it's sixty degrees outside, and you're not getting in any water." I pour dry Cheerios in her bowl as Miles chomps down on a jelly bagel.

"Dante, come eat something!" I yell, bending to pet Powder's head as he clears his food bowl. "We gotta be outta here in ten minutes so we can meet Omari at the gate." I wash my hands, grab a tangerine, and gather the bags to load up the car. But before I walk over to the key ring, I review my plan for the tenth time. It's a fifteen-minute drive to the park, we'll hop on a few rides before Hailee shows up, grab a bite to eat, see a show, ride a few more rides, get a treat, be in the car by 5:15 p.m. at the latest, and home by 5:30 p.m. Nothing could go wrong. I've covered all my bases. I grab the keys and stuff them into my jeans pocket.

◊◊◊

"I thought you'd get sick of being forced on all those kiddie rides," I say to Hailee as we pass the Mind Eraser on the red, blue, and gray Whistlestop Train.

Zion took Dante, Bailey, and Miles for snacks to give Hailee and me some time alone. I chose the train so we'd finally be able to talk. The rickety train travels no faster than twelve miles per hour around the entirety of the park, and this is our second trip. All day long, I waited for Hailee to scream how sick she was of spending our time on the teacups, flying carousel, and bumper cars, but she let the kids drag us to each ride without a single complaint.

Hailee laughs. "Oh, the only reason I agreed to come was because I knew we'd stick to the kiddie rides! I remember that story you told me about you and Ariana going on that roller coaster with the three-hundred-foot drop and loopty loops every five seconds. No way you were getting me on anything faster than those tea-cups! I was so dizzy afterward."

I laugh with my head thrown back and get curious eyes from two adults a few carts ahead of us.

"Well, now that I know you have the same thrill tolerance as Dante, I'll be sure to keep any future dates outside of amusement parks."

Her eyes light up. "Ah, so this *was* our second date?"

I scoot closer until we're hip to hip and arch my left brow dramatically. "What? You couldn't tell when I hauled Miles over my shoulder so we could all run and find a potty in time?"

Hailee smirks at me, suppressing a laugh. "You know, Novah, you're a lot of things, but I think funny may be at the top of the list."

"Oh, well, now you gotta give me the top three."

She sits up straighter, facing me. "Number one, as established—you're funny."

I purse my lips, nodding vigorously, and my locs fall in my face.

"Two. You're like responsible as hell."

I suck in a breath, scrunching my face. "Ooh, I think a lot of people would disagree with that one."

"And three," she says, shifting the hair out of my eye. "You're thoughtful and kind. And I love that."

"And you are outrageously sweet, smart as hell, caring to a fault, and literally the prettiest person I've ever met," I whisper back to her.

"That's four." Hailee's eyes are suddenly serious, asking a question, and I nod my head just the slightest bit.

In the shadows of the clouds, her face is so close that I can smell the warm cocoa and florals in her body mist. My heart beats uncontrollably as she leans in—and I find my eyes laser focused on her full lips until they flow onto mine. The hairs on my arms stand on end as I rest my palm at the base of her neck, tilting my head to welcome her more fully. Hailee's anxious hands find my thighs as she presses her soft lips more fervently, and I let each of my senses be consumed by her. I don't know how much time has passed, but the train's loud hoot sounds twice and we draw apart as we pull into the station.

◊◊◊

"Guys, I need you to keep up," I say, trying to keep my voice level as we walk through the turnstile to exit the park.

By the time Hailee and I got off the train, a couple things had happened. I officially had a girlfriend, her ride was already outside waiting, it was already 5:15 p.m., and the orangish-yellow tone of the evening sky I usually love was starting to freak me out. But Zion wasn't answering the phone. By 5:40, in a mild panic and by chance alone, I found them in a crowd taking pictures with Looney Tunes characters. The sun was barely lighting the cloudy sky anymore. Apparently, Zi's phone had died and he didn't see what the big rush was anyways. That's because he's catching a ride home with Omari after they clock out and has no clue I plan to drive the four of us back.

I'm almost at the car with Miles bopping on my hip before I realize I don't hear the squeak of Bailey's shoes right behind me anymore. She's about fifteen feet back and fumbling with her laces while trying to shoo Dante's attempts to help.

I run back toward them, place Miles down, and bend at her side. But before I can reach out, she angrily signs, "I can do it!" And I resolve to wait as patiently as I can with folded arms and my sneakers tapping the asphalt at triple speed.

The three minutes we stand there waiting is enough to lose the last bit of sunlight. But it really doesn't matter now, considering I've been stuck in this parking spot for the last ten minutes. My phone hasn't started vibrating with Ari's angry calls and texts yet, but I know I'm getting closer to my doom by the second.

"Didn't you say Ari wanted us home before it got dark?" Dante asks from the passenger seat of the SUV.

My fingers are wrapped so tightly around the steering wheel to keep them from shaking that the blood has stopped flowing to the tips. I've had very little real experience driving in the dark.

"Well, it's nighttime, and you're still not driving," he says, cutting into my thoughts.

"Right, right," I mutter, flexing my fingers. I look at Miles and Bailey strapped into their car seats, snoring in the back. And reach over to ensure Dante's seat belt is locked in place too. A couple deep breaths and I turn on my headlights and put the car in drive. It's now or never.

Like Daddy always complimented, I really am the best at following the rules of the road. I don't have a "need for speed" like Zion, and I'm not an aggressive driver like Ari, so the first few minutes are smooth sailing. Well, besides the woman who cut me off and gave me the finger at an intersection when I clearly had the right of way.

After that, I decide to take the back roads to play it safe. We're only five minutes from the house, and still no missed calls from Ari—perfect plan, perfect day. I turn on Lincoln Parkway, squinting as a car on the other side of the road comes toward us, blinding me with its high beams. My heart races, but I do what I was taught, keeping my hands at ten to two and reducing my speed until the car passes. There are no cars behind me anyways.

"Asshole," I mutter as my eyes adjust again to the night road. When my heart returns to its regular beat, I find the courage to press on the gas and then... something flies into the road. I jerk the steering wheel right, jutting my arm out over Dante's chest, and slam my foot on the brakes—the road vanishes, tires squeal, glass shatters, screams, and there's a sickening crunch as we crash into the guardrail.

My fingers have a death grip on the steering wheel when my frantic eyes fly open seconds later. I turn slowly, seeing Dante's and Bailey's panicked expressions as Miles wails in the back seat. But there are no visible scratches, no blood, no airbags deployed. Only the sound of my phone faintly ringing.

"Is everyone okay?" I pant, moving to unbuckle my seat belt. Dante follows my lead, squeaking out a small "Yes" as I hop up, reaching back to unclip Bailey from her booster seat. She climbs forward and into Dante's arms. "Go stand on the side of the road." I climb in the back, where Miles is still crying, unbuckle him, and grab him in my arms before exiting too. I place him on the grass, his body still trembling as sobs overtake his body, but physically he's okay. Physically, we're all okay. We hold hands, careful to stay out of the road, as we walk toward the front of the car, and then I see it.

I see what I caused. The bumper of our new car is banged up and hanging off one side. Both headlights are busted; there's a flat tire and shattered glass on the ground from the missing side mirror.

I look at my baby siblings and their wide eyes, attempting to steady my breath even as my mind races. I did this. I crashed the car. It's all over now. The judge is going to see what I did and social services will take us away from one another. Who knows where they'll send us all? Maybe Miles and Bailey will stay together, but what if they don't know ASL? What if Miles's foster parents beat kids for wetting the bed? Who's gonna keep Dante after his first night terror rocks their home? What's gonna stop Korey from running away from some teen group home the first chance he gets? What if one of them gets lost in the system and it's all my fault?

"That deer came outta nowhere," Dante says, looking up at me, but I'm clutching at my chest now, scratching the skin where it feels like my heart is ready to jump out.

I open my mouth to speak, but it feels like the air has been vacuumed from my throat, strangling the sob that wants so badly to escape. I did this. The realization that I could've killed them sets in, and I'm on my knees, willing Mama's face to appear in front of me.

"Novah," I hear one of them say. But my eyes won't let me focus and my chest burns. Music rings from somewhere nonstop as my face meets the ground.

I think I'm gonna pass out, when I feel my hair being tugged, raising my head out of the grass. Dante's mumbled voice comes from a distance, and then someone's small hands are on my clammy cheeks. With their every exhale comes a rush of air on my face, and I welcome it until my breathing is in sync with theirs. My eyes fly open. Bailey's big, calm eyes are in front of me. She's nodding as my heart slows. She continues the action, rubbing my face with her cool palm and holding up her sky-blue bracelet in my view for I don't know how long before headlights shine in my peripheral vision. I think the car's going to pass us, but it slows yards away.

Doors open, feet pound on the asphalt, and I look their way only because Bailey does first. It's Ari, Zion, and Korey running toward us. I will myself to stand, feeling instantly relieved at the sight of them, despite what they're about to learn. Bailey doesn't let go of my hand.

CHAPTER 18

Ari, Zion, and Korey arrived back at the house at the same time to find us and the car missing. They didn't have to wonder where we were for long, because Dante called, sent them our location, and assured them that no one was hurt. When he got off the phone, he comforted Miles, while Bailey brought me down and taught me how to breathe again.

What did I do? Ruin everything.

Mr. Johnston drives us home, our busted SUV trailing behind on the quiet road.

"I'll come back and give it a full look over tomorrow for you, Ari," he says from the front door. "It's fixable, but it may take a minute. Don't worry, I'll fit you in my schedule." She closes the door behind him, turning to us with an unreadable expression on her face.

I sit on the couch, running a hand over Powder's soft coat, with Zion and Korey sitting on either side of me. Bailey, Miles, and Dante went down for bed about thirty minutes ago. It's time to face her.

I hold my breath as Ari walks over, every footstep pounding in my ear until she lands in front of me, arms crossed over her pink hoodie. But she doesn't say anything, just stares down at me, fuming.

I sit up on the couch, nudging Powder off my lap. He circles his bed, settling in, and I run a nervous hand over my locs, finding Ari's eyes again. All their eyes are on me.

But mine fall, finding the tiger's-eye bracelet on my wrist. I can't stand to look at them, so I fidget with the *N* charm instead, wishing Mama and Daddy were here. I never would've done something like this if they were still here.

"Ari, I've never driven in the dark by myself before" is all I'm able to get out.

Her tone is level, but I can tell it's taking all her effort not to scream. "Yeah, I'm aware of that. But you still drove. Funny, huh? Isn't it, guys?" she says, looking around and flapping her arms in the air. "You've barely *ever* driven by yourself, but you drove anyways. Nobody told you you could take the car. You didn't have permission to take the car. But you didn't care about any of that!" she shrieks, completely abandoning the calm act. "You just knew there was something Novah wanted to do, so with complete disregard for any of our rules, you packed your baby siblings in a car and still put the keys in the ignition!"

"I didn't mean for this to happen! The drive this morning was easy. But then I lost track of time and it was dark. I was nervous, but I thought if I drove carefully, then—"

"Nov," Zion cuts in, "why didn't you tell me that at the park?"

I hesitate. My reasoning seems silly now. "Because if I told you, then you'd know I took the car in the first place."

"So you'd rather put all of you in harm's way than admit you were wrong?" Ari asks.

"No!"

"And let me guess why you lost track of time," she says, cocking her head to the side. "Would it have anything to do with that little girl you conveniently left off the schedule today?"

I swallow hard.

"Yeah, that's what I thought. It was a mistake hiring her; you've been nothing but trouble since I did."

"And what does that mean?"

"It means that she's about to get fired and you're to blame." Ari turns on her heel, heading for the kitchen, and I'm right behind her, yelling too now.

"You can't do that!"

"Watch me!"

Mr. Crane bangs on the wall, and suddenly Powder's

on his feet, barking madly in the direction the sound came from.

"Ari, I shouldn't have taken the car. That was my bad, but what good would firing Hailee do? What are you punishing her for?"

"I'm punishing *you*, Novah," she screams, slamming her hands on the counter. "You're the one who messed up. You risked everything tonight!"

My voice falters. "I—I can't help that a deer jumped in the road."

"It doesn't matter what you couldn't help after the fact! You shouldn't have taken the car in the first place. Now none of us can get around!"

"Oh, and there it is!" I say, letting my hands fall with a slap to my thighs.

She rolls her eyes, heading back into the living room and plopping on the couch. Zion and Korey sit where we left them, looking bored while we hash it out.

"There what is?" she asks.

"The truth!" I say, with folded arms. "You're not *really* worried about us or the car. You're worried about being able to get around for yourself so you can keep hanging out with your little friends!"

Ari hops off the couch—the change in her eyes is menacing as she gets in my face. "Are you being serious right now?"

"If you weren't so selfish with the car and

everything else, none of this would've happened in the first place."

Ari pushes me, and I bump into the altar, jostling the items off the shelf. I don't give myself a full chance to recover before I push her back, hearing a loud "whoa" from Zion as Ari grabs a fistful of my hair, and then I'm scratching at whatever part of her my wild hands land on. We go at it for only a few seconds before the altar comes crashing down. I'm raging and out of breath, Korey has my hands pinned behind my back, and Zion's arms are wrapped around Ari, pulling her hair to get her off me.

Powder barks, jumping at our feet, and I know there's no way the kids can have slept through that.

"Y'all need to calm down," Zion yells as we both still move to get at each other again. I flip my hair back and find Ari's eyes somehow surpass my own rage.

"How could you say that to me?!" she yells, her face contorting in fury.

"Because it's true."

"Yesterday was the first time I've seen my high school friends in months, Novah. I went up to Howard with Lexi and Erica because *they* convinced me that I needed a break, and they were right!"

I snort. "A break from what?"

"You," she spits. "You and the shop. My responsibilities and . . . school."

I squint at her as she pushes Zion's hands away. He looks confused too.

"School?"

"Yes, school," she sighs. "I've been taking business and marketing classes at the community college for the last few months. If we're gonna make it, I have to learn how to run Lively's the right way. And that means that I have homework and tests that I need to study for and occasionally, I'll go to the library to try and catch up on work and get so caught up that I lose track of time!"

Korey's grip slackens, and my arms fall to my sides.

"Those friends you're talking about," she says angrily, pushing up her sleeves, "are my study groups, and I'm not going to apologize for it either. I'm allowed to do something for myself, and if it doesn't mean endangering yourself or the kids, then you are too, Novah! But I will not allow you to put them in harm's way. You don't get to risk their lives or their futures no matter what you think of me or my rules or my decisions!"

I stare around, looking at Korey and Zion, for I don't know what—confirmation? But I know she's telling the truth.

"Ari, I'm—"

"Don't bother," she says, with a finger to the bridge of her nose.

I open my mouth to try and say something again,

but there are three hard knocks at the door and all of our minds race to the same conclusion—a surprise visit from Ms. Lusby.

We all scramble to clean up as quickly as we can. Zion and I lift the TV stand and push it back against the wall. Ari drops to the floor, stacking broken frames and hiding soil from a broken pot under the carpet while Korey pushes the couch back in place, before running to Powder and leading the barking dog to his cage.

Another round of knocks at the door sound, and the place doesn't look much better, but it's the best we can do.

Ari takes a deep breath, shaking her arms and legs out, and wrenches the door open to two tall officers scanning us and the room with serious expressions.

"We're responding to a noise complaint filed by a neighbor," the first officer, with a shining bald head, says. "This is the Wilkinson residence, correct?"

I stand frozen, my heart beating out of my chest as my eyes shoot toward the wall. Did Mr. Crane hear everything we'd just admitted from his home? I remember him telling Daddy once that he could only ever make out muffled voices coming from our house. But he had to have heard everything this time. We were so loud. Maybe they already know what I did? They must be here to take us from Ari. I swipe at a burning tear rolling down my cheek. I thought we'd have more time.

I pray that Ari will look back at me with some sort of reassurance in her eyes, but she stays forward, pulling her hoodie up on her shoulder to hide the scratches I just put there. Even worse, she's completely silent.

"Yes, sir, we're the Wilkinsons," Zion says, walking forward to stand beside Ari. "We just had a little argument," he says, looking confused. "And our dog"—he points to Powder in his cage, now giving quiet yelps—"gets a little rowdy every now and then. But there's nothing happening that would warrant a 9-1-1 call."

The bald officer looks between Zion and Ari, while his mustached partner silently observes me and Korey and the rest of the room from the door. I give a sheepish grin. They can't see the broken glass and lumpy carpet behind the couch where they stand. I pray they don't ask to take a look inside.

"Can I speak to you all's guardian?" he asks.

"That's me," Ari says, snapping to her senses. "I'm eighteen, the guardian and owner of this house." She reaches for her wallet on the stand. "I have my ID right here."

The bald cop checks it out. "It's just me and my siblings here," she said. "There's seven of us, plus our dog.

So things do get a bit hectic sometimes, but we promise this won't happen again."

"Huh. You two could be twins," he comments, his eyes flitting to me. He hands Ari her ID. "All right. And what about that car in the driveway?"

Ari leans forward, peering out the door as if she doesn't know what they're talking about. "Oh, right! That's kind of what we were discussing when you all arrived."

My eyes shoot to the back of Ari's head. Is she about to rat me out to actual cops? What if she's decided she's done putting up with my mess and realized that I'm not worth the trouble? Maybe tonight's the night she realizes it would be easier to just put me in the system rather than risk that all of the other kids be in the same position. I feel a sudden wave of nausea overtake me and sway, but luckily no one notices.

"I was driving home on a back road close by when a deer shot out in the road." She chuckles nervously. And I release a breath. "Somehow the guardrail was unharmed, but our car wasn't so lucky."

"Not on Lincoln Parkway?" the officer with a mustache asks.

"Actually, yeah. That was where it happened."

"Ahh, I see. Same thing happened to my brother-in-law last year, except he broke his arm and nose. You really gotta watch out for those deer this time of year.

Make sure you drive slow and keep your eyes peeled for 'em."

"Well, we're happy to hear you're okay," the bald officer says, resting his hands on his belt. "Everything checks out here. But try and keep the noise down in the future so we don't have to come back. Have a good night."

I release a breath and hear Zion exhale too when they turn to walk down the steps. Ari closes the door behind them with her head held down, grumbling to herself.

"Ari," Zion starts, but she holds up a finger silencing him as she moves to the window, peeking behind the curtains.

"Are you okay?" Korey asks, looking concerned too.

But she slashes a *zip it* sign in the air as she opens the blinds.

I hear the officers start their car and pull away, but her hand is still hanging in the air as she mumbles, and I'm able to make out the sounds. She's counting. I exchange a nervous look with Korey because when she reaches thirty, she pushes herself away from the window and heads out the front door.

"What are you doing?" Zion calls, following her out. "Y'all stay right here," he says to me and Korey when we reach the front porch.

We watch as Ari bangs on Mr. Crane's door double-fisted as Zion stares in disbelief at the foot of the steps.

Mr. Crane yanks his door open, mouth poised to yell, but Ari beats him to it.

"What the hell is wrong with you?" she screams in the man's face. "I know it was you who called!"

"I sure did." He nods, without a hint of remorse. "The hell is wrong *witch'all* making all that noise so late at night."

"It's seven thirty. You old asshole!"

"It's seven thirty and y'all are goin' about like you ain't got no sense! Now you got that dog barking waking me up at all hours of the night. It's either that dog or one of you yelling or stomping around interruptin' me, my sleep, and my shows."

"I don't give a damn about you or your sleep, Crane," she says, taking a step forward into his house. She's in his face now, gesturing wildly, and I'm scared that at any second, she'll hit the man. "Stay away from me and my family, and the next time you pick up the phone to call the cops and get in our business, you're gonna have me to deal with."

Zion rushes up the steps, pushing Ari away from his door as she yells all types of obscenities. Mr. Crane slams his door shut, but she's unhinged, cursing nonstop until Zion can get her back inside the house.

Ari falls on the couch, now quiet, with her face in

her hands and trembling like Miles did after the accident.

I've never seen Ari lose it like that before. She's never put her hands on me. Out of all of us, she's almost always the calmest—the levelheaded one. It was me. I pushed her too far this time. And my heart hurts, watching my sister fall apart like this.

I bend at the foot of the couch in front of Ari as she sits unmoving, her breath coming in quick shallow beats. I pull her hand down, revealing a tortured expression, smudged tears, and scared eyes. This is how she looked the night of our parents' accident. When she finally came to our room to check on me, I couldn't produce a single word, so she climbed in and held me, wordlessly.

"Do you really think I care anything about that car?" she asks, sniffling. "Do you really think I fought for custody because I wanted some kind of sick praise?"

I shake my head quickly, remembering what I'd yelled at her outside of Korey's school that day. Those words don't feel right anymore. Looking at Ari's face now, I can't believe I ever had the gall to think it, and I hate that I believed it.

"Good," she whispers. "Because I don't care about the car or any kind of adoration, and it *sucks* that you think that about me, Novah. It's your life. It's you and Dante and Bailey and Miles— Your lives are what I care about. The four of you could've been killed tonight. Do you get that yet?" She swallows hard, eyes pleading with me to hear her. "You all could've died in a car accident just like Mama and Daddy, of all ways. And then where would that leave me, Korey, and Zion, huh? That would devastate us. What would we do without y'all?"

She's right. Antoinette was right too. I've been too hard on Ari. I couldn't fathom losing any of my siblings. I forgot how to breathe tonight when I realized that I might've done just that. But that's not what I was thinking about this morning. I don't know what I was thinking. "I didn't realize . . . I didn't think like that when I—"

"No, you didn't, but every time I get behind the wheel, that's what I think about. Leaving and not being able to come home to you guys. I can barely hold it together when Zion needs the car." Zion throws an arm over her shaking shoulders, and Korey sits on the edge of the couch, placing a hand over hers. "I've thought about everything that led up to the night Mama and Daddy died a million times. You were right to call me selfish the day I tried to get you and Zion to work in my place. If I'd never asked, they'd still be here."

"Whoa." Zion's eyes widen as he forces Ari's eyes onto his and says firmly, "That's not on you."

I bite my lip, looking up at them. "It's not on you, Ari. It was my plan to get us all the night off."

"And I bitched that day, just as much as y'all did," he says, shaking his head. "That doesn't make anything that happened that night our fault."

Ari nods to herself, like she's willing herself to believe his words. "My point is, is that I've been selfish my whole life, because I could afford to be with Mama and Daddy and especially with you three picking up my slack. But when they died, I promised them to put you all first in every way. I'm not perfect and I make mistakes, but every time you throw that word in my face again"—she inhales deeply—"it reminds me of how I'm failing them, Novah."

My mouth falls open, but I'm speechless. Those weren't my intentions. But then I think of how many times I've called her selfish, with malice in my voice. How many times I've thought just that exactly. I'm horrified—maybe they were my intentions. Korey kicks my leg, making a face urging me to say something to make her feel better. But how do I explain myself? What excuses purposely making Ari feel that bad about herself, just because of how awful I've felt?

"I'm so sorry, Ari," I start softly. "I know you love us and I know you're trying every day. I just . . . I don't know." I shrug. "I haven't been thinking things through lately. But I don't want you to feel like Mama and Daddy wouldn't be proud of you. You're doing us all the greatest favor by keeping us together. I know that. And I wouldn't ask you to apologize for taking those classes either." She finally looks up at me, wiping her nose with the sleeve of her Howard sweatshirt. "You deserved to do things that make you happy."

Ari lunges forward, and I think she's attacking me again. But then her arms wrap around my neck and I feel myself soften.

"Let's make a deal," I say when she pulls back, because I finally know what I can say to make at least a small part of this better. "You keep going to school. I'll call Trinity about setting up a day to shadow her, and when one of the four of us needs help with something," I say, looking at Korey and Zion too, "maybe we open our mouths and ask."

They nod in unison.

"And I want us all to stop hiding stuff from one another. It's a waste of time," Korey says.

"What are you hiding?" Ari asks with an arched brow.

"Me?" he says, pointing to his chest. "Oh, nothing. Out of the four of us, I'm doing the best. I meant you hiding that you were going to school. That was dumb. Novah running around stealing people's keys and cars and Zion stealing that money outta the register and then putting it back without saying anything."

Ari slaps his arm. "That was you?!"

He winces. "Nov, you told him?"

"In confidence!" I glare at Korey.

"It's fine!" Ari says before we can start arguing. "I agree with Korey. No more secrets. No more slacking. No more pushing through alone."

CHAPTER 19

I unbuckle Miles from his booster seat in the Uber XL and he latches himself onto my hip as we pile the dirty bags of laundry on the sidewalk. Mr. Johnston said our car would take at least another week before it was ready. He's working on it basically for free and only in between his true clients, so we had no room to complain.

"Dante, grab one of those bags," Ari tells him as she unlocks the door to Lively's and flips the switch.

We weren't technically supposed to be open today, but we woke up this morning with no electricity and Zion saying, "I knew I was forgetting something."

With no Wi-Fi, an empty fridge (because I'd chosen to catch up on homework instead of grocery shopping yesterday), and laundry overflowing out of every room, it was just easier to come into the shop and use the electricity and perfectly functioning washer and dryer than stay home in the dark. Our dryer at home never really worked properly anyways, especially not since Zion watched a couple YouTube videos and decided to take the repair work into his own hands.

It's been a few days since the night of the car accident, and Ari and I made up. Not like last time where we played nice in front of the kids—even though we could never even do that convincingly. This time I plan to take Ari, her rules—and faith that she's trying a whole lot harder than I ever gave her credit for—seriously. And she's promised to be the sister I can lean on.

I sit at the front reception desk, scrawling out a grocery list with Bailey on my lap and Miles coloring beside us as Ari takes a mop to the checkered floor. Korey, Dante, and Zion are in the back playing some raucous game with Powder and the four walk-in dogs that have been dropped off for day care today.

"Do you guys wanna come with me to Acosta's or stay here?" I ask Bailey and Miles, who immediately jump out of their seats and start pulling their shoes and coats on.

Ari hands me the card, and we're about to leave when the bell dings behind me and she smiles politely.

"Mr. Lane, nice to see you again," she says kindly, bending to pet the bug-eyed Boston terrier on the leash, "and it's nice to see you too, Bacon!"

I grimace at Mr. Lane before my eyes land on Bacon, who's already barking maniacally at my feet. I don't dislike a ton of dogs, but Bacon's one of them. Mr. Lane swears he's potty trained, but he always has accidents aimed conveniently at my shoes, growls whenever Miles gets too close, and loves to start fights with all the smaller dogs in his day care room.

Miles climbs scared into my arms just as Bacon starts the growling. I'm thankful that at least I don't have to be the one to deal with Mr. Lane or his funny-looking dog today. "All righty. We're gonna head out," I say, stepping around them, pulling Bailey behind us.

"Actually, Novah," Mr. Lane says, before I can reach the door, "I was hoping to run into you today."

I turn back with dread at his closed-mouth grin and know he's up to no good. Since the day he tried using Mama and Daddy against me, I'd done everything possible to ensure he had no reason to single me out or even the chance to speak to me alone. That sometimes meant blatantly ignoring him and rushing out of the room when he'd call my name, making sure to have his work done (sometimes early), and showing up to his classes on time. I'd even scored an eighty-eight on his last quiz. So, if he isn't here strictly to talk dog business, then it must be to cause trouble.

All I'm able to muster is a flat "Oh?"

"Yes, and I'd like for you to be a part of the conversation too, Ari," he says gravely.

Ari straightens, mimicking his serious look. "Did Novah do something wrong?"

"As a matter of fact, she did."

I sigh and tell Bailey and Miles to go play in the back with the boys. Mr. Lane has such horrible timing. Why did he have to come in here today when Ari and I were still trying to get our relationship back on track? And why did she ask if I did something wrong and not, "Were you being an asshole as usual, causing my sister to act in some way she normally wouldn't?"

"What's goin' on?" Ari asks, looking concerned. "Novah told me her grade in World History was picking up."

Mr. Lane nods. "Yes, and it is. But I feel it's important to make sure that we can keep it that way. I've been meaning to send you an email about a little discussion Novah and I had a few weeks back in regard to a failed test and a few missing assignments—"

"I turned in all of those assignments already," I say, looking at Ari instead of him.

"Where she was very disrespectful and stormed off while we were in the middle of a discussion about her academics." He pauses, waiting for me to disagree with him, but I don't bother. Mr. Lane didn't see me prepping to launch a textbook at his head, so I guess I'm technically getting off easy.

"While Novah has succeeded in catching up and turning her grade in my class around in a short amount of time, she's managed to do so in the most disrespectful way possible."

Ari's eyes squint as she looks from Mr. Lane. "How?"

"Blatant disregard and intentionally bad artwork." My eyes drop to the floor as I try to disguise my smile. Every paper that I'd turned in to him since that day had at least one of my badly drawn illustrations of Mr. Lane, sometimes highlighting his patchy beard, beady eyes, or the occasional caption about his horrible coffee breath. I fully expected to eventually be called into Principal Jay's office, where he claimed bullying or some nonsense. Even though he'd started this. But he's gone the direct route to rat me out to Ari.

"I don't know what that means," Ari says, shrugging, "but let's go back. Why did you storm off while Mr. Lane was speaking to you?"

"I—"

"I was giving your sister a pep talk," he says, cutting me off, "about the importance of goals and proper motivation. So I offered up some options and suggested that she try and make your parents proud."

Ari goes rigid, and her eyes are suddenly doing that frightening bulging thing, and I deflate until she turns, aiming them at Mr. Lane. Not me?

He pauses, every bit of worry clouding his eyes.

"What did you say to her?" she asks, taking a step toward him. Mr. Lane's at least five foot ten, but right now, Ari feels taller.

"I simply asked her," he says with a nervous chuckle, "to try and make . . ." But his voice fades as her head cocks to the side.

"You asked my grieving sister to try and make our dead parents proud? That's what you just said," Ari says, nodding. "You tried to guilt a child into using her parents' tragic passing, a few mere months ago, as some kind of sick motivation technique in your World History class. Not because you care about Novah, her well-being, or her grades, I'm sure. As a matter of fact, I don't know why you thought you could speak to my sister like that, and there's no excuse, but I promise you it was the last time, Mr. Lane. My parents were proud of Novah, every day of their lives, and in their physical absence I am proud of Novah for helping to keep our family stable, putting our little siblings first always, and for simply being." I don't know when it happened, but Ari somehow managed to back Mr. Lane into the entrance. When his back hits the door, he and Bacon jump in unison, startled by the bells, and turn to leave in a huff. But not before Ari says, "I'll see you in Principal Jay's office Monday morning. Eight a.m."

I bite my bottom lip, about ready to burst at the seams. That was everything I'd ever wanted to say to Mr. Lane and everything I'd ever wanted to hear all wrapped in one. I wanna cry and laugh and hug her all at the same time, but when she turns, all I can do is smirk. "You like me, don't you?" I say playfully.

Her scowl finally breaks into a full-fledged smile. "Only a little bit," she says, holding her thumb and pointer finger a pinch apart.

But when the doorbell rings, my heart leaps into my throat.

It's Ms. Lusby.

"Ariana," she says sternly. "We need to discuss a few things. Starting with an important call I received."

Ari looks like a deer caught in headlights, so I take a step forward, trying to muster courage though it feels like my limbs are suddenly made of Jell-O.

My voice is shaky when I ask, "What call?"

"One from your neighbor, Mr. Joseph Crane," she says with pursed lips.

"He's a liar!" I shout before I can stop myself.

"Novah, you don't know what he's said yet."

"It doesn't matter." I can already feel the sweat gathering on my forehead as my panic rises. "That man has always hated us even before we lost our parents! And there's two sides to every story, Ms. Lusby."

"He claims that an argument caused some fight to break out in your home a few days ago. Possibly a physical one?" Her penetrating eyes look from Ari to me. "When the noise didn't stop, he called 9-1-1 to report a disturbance and claims that after the cops left, you"—she nods at Ariana—"came to his home, cursed him out, and had to be removed from his front steps by your brother. Now, your custody hearing is supposed to be in less than two months, but it looks like we'll have to start making arrangements before then. Especially if I'm not given 'your side' soon. Would either of you care to explain?"

My mouth opens, then closes as I fight the urge to burst into tears. We were supposed to have more time to prepare—more time to get better together. But I can already hear the judge slamming his gavel and declaring Ari as an unsuitable guardian, when nothing could be further from the truth. Without one another we never would've survived losing Mama and Daddy. They taught us how to survive together, to lean on one another, and now the state could turn around with the full expectation that we can't make it on our own?

Just the thought of seeing my siblings lined up with suitcases in hand as we're driven away from Ari one by one makes my stomach churn. I purse my lips together now, trying to slow my breath even as my heart beats erratically in my chest, tears burn the back of my eyes, and panic and fear fight to come out on top.

This is my fault.

Ms. Lusby wouldn't even be here if I hadn't been so stupid, and now I don't know the words that will stop her from making the decision that will wreck our lives forever. How did I ever think we'd gotten away with it and could just move on peacefully when so many things went wrong?

I can tell from the grave look in Ms. Lusby's eyes that we weren't even close.

Ari was right. I *was* selfish. And because of me, this is it.

Ms. Lusby gives us a heavy exhale before taking the nearest seat in our waiting area. She places her briefcase on the checkered floor and gestures for us to sit in the open seats in front of her, and we do. I catch Ariana wiping her tears with the sleeve of her lavender hoodie and take her hand in mine, before turning forward. We tried, but it wasn't good enough. Silently, I send one million apologies up to Mama and Daddy. This is the worst way we could have failed them.

CHAPTER 20

I fidget on the small couch in Dr. Stone's office, squished between Korey and Ariana. Miles, Bailey, Dante, and Zion sit on the adjacent couch, and Dr. Stone faces us all in her own chair, cross-legged with a notepad on her lap.

Lucky for us, Mr. Crane didn't clearly hear our fight, and it turns out that Ms. Lusby was more worried about Ari's outburst with Mr. Crane and the arguing going on within our own home. Without contention, we agreed to the court-ordered therapy twice a week. Considering the alternative, we were getting off easy.

It seemed like it'd be a huge waste of time, though. We were all finally chipping in equally and getting along. Zion hadn't missed a shift. I opened my mouth and asked Ari for help with the kids when I needed it. I was caught up on schoolwork. Ari wasn't schooling in hiding, and for those five days, I was prouder of my family than I have been in a long time.

After basic introductions and a "Why are we here?"

conversation, the first hour of our session with Dr. Stone focused on conflict resolution. Now she's trying to dig deeper.

"So, you all have given me some surface info about your parents. I know what they did for a living, how they raised you all and juggled seven kids and a dog shop. But I feel like there's a lot missing from the picture that made you all who you were with them, and who you all are now."

She sits back in her chair, surveying us. "I mean, I know that their pictures are up everywhere, you all are continuing their legacy and work, doing what you need to stay together, but when's the last time you guys sat together and reminisced—you know, when's the last time you guys traded stories or shared memories about them? Ari?"

She shakes her head with a shrug.

"Dante?"

He does the same. I touch my finger to the crystals on my wrist, biting on my lip with the word *never* teetering on my tongue.

But Korey speaks up, leaning forward on his knees. "We've literally never done that before."

Dr. Stone's brows rise into her hairline. "Never? Really?" She places her notepad on the circle glass table beside her, uncrossing her legs in the process. "Guys, your parents passed *six months ago*."

"We know that," Ari snaps, and then immediately looks like she regrets her words. "Sorry," she whispers.

Dr. Stone waves her apology away. "I know you do." She nods. "And I wasn't trying to be insensitive. No one knows that better than you all. What I'm saying is that you do a disservice not only to your ancestors but to yourselves by not using your time, your thoughts, and your breath to speak life into their names. Have you all visited their resting place yet?"

I swallow hard but shake my head no when none of my siblings respond.

"Because it would be painful, right? I get that. And it's something that you guys can work toward if you'd like to. But processing and fully healing usually doesn't come through pretending you're okay. It's crucial that you guys have these talks."

"Why?" I ask. "Why is it so important for us to have to say out loud what we all remember and experienced?"

Dr. Stone rests her chin in her hand, pointing two fingers at Miles and Bailey. "Because of them. Most kids don't start forming memories until they're, what, two or three years old? That means you, Ari, Zion, Korey, and even Dante have an advantage. The things you guys remember, the lessons your parents taught you, their practices, their love . . . Miles and Bailey didn't get the time you guys have. There are things that they will forget—things they didn't even get the chance to be taught that the rest of you did. You keep Lisa and Ezekiel alive for yourselves and Miles and Bailey by speaking life into these memories." She snaps up with a full smile, clapping her hands together. "All right, so . . . who's first?"

"First to what?" Dante asks.

"Share a memory! I'm interested to hear more. What about you?" she asks, tickling Bailey's and Miles's stomachs. They both laugh, and then Bailey sits up, nodding. Her big eyes look at each of us, waiting to hear what we have to say.

But I'm at a loss for words. I have a thousand memories of Mama and Daddy, but I haven't had to do this before. When I do think of them, I always see Mama bent at the altar or whipping up her famous secret crab dip or, when I was younger, guiding me through my anxieties. When I think of Daddy, I see him running around the playroom with dogs, writing in his journal at his desk, or telling me I'm beautiful. Since they've died, I've only spoken of them in passing, about their death. Or about what their deaths did to our family. How do I put those memories into words after so long?

Miles hops off Zion's lap, cheesing and fidgeting with the tail of his gray sweater. "I remember stuff."

"Do you?" Dr. Stone beams. "Well, I think it'll be great if we hear from you first! What do you remember?"

His eyes find mine, and I give him a small smile, nodding for him to go on.

"I remember," he starts again, "when we'd come home from school and me and Daddy played Spider-Man beats up the Black Panther."

Dante chuckles, and we all exchange nervous smiles.

"And was that fun?" Dr. Stone asks.

He nods quickly. "And now I get to play with Zi, and we have fun too!"

Zion grabs Miles up from behind, kissing him on his cheek, and he bursts into a thousand giggles.

"Great start," Dr. Stone says. "Who's next?"

Dante raises his head, and Dr. Stone points to him. "Mama liked hearing me talk about dinosaurs." He shrugs.

"Oh, I didn't know you were into paleontology."

He smiles widely. "I am. And she thought they were cool too, when she learned about them as a kid! She took me to the library to find books about them and even read them with me sometimes. Daddy didn't like reading the books, but he knew all my favorites and last summer we built a Lego *Tyrannosaurus rex* together. It took us a whole month to finish. They think"—his smile lessens—"they thought that I could be a paleontologist or archaeologist when I grow up if I really want to."

"And do you still want to?"

"Mmm, maybe, or I could be an astronaut. I like space too."

The room's quiet for a while as Dr. Stone waits for someone else to speak, and I'm surprised to hear Ari clear her throat. I turn to face her.

"Daddy never thought anything I wanted to do or liked was stupid. I mean, maybe he did, but he didn't show it." She looks down, fidgeting with her fingers, and bites her lip. "He took me and my friends to the midnight premieres of that five-movie vampire saga, he watched reality TV shows with me, and when I decided I hated the flute after school one day and picked up a volleyball for the first time, Daddy was there. He explained each position to me and told me before I even tried that I'd probably be great as a libero. He was right."

Zion scratches at the stubble on his chin, speaking without needing a prompt. "Daddy's the reason I got my first and only girlfriend, Isabella," he chuckles to himself. "Turns out she's horrible, but at the time I liked her—like, desperately. But I didn't have game and he knew it, so he told me to go the 'sweet' route. We'd talked before a little in English class, and I knew she loved poetry. So he sat me down, helped me write out two stanzas about her eyes, and then we went to the supermarket and I picked out this rainbow bouquet. He said she would either see the effort I put into all of this and appreciate it or slam the door in my face, but there was only one way to find out. So he drove me to her house and ducked down in the car, watching while I wheezed through the poem." He pushes his glasses up the bridge of his nose, shaking his head with a grin. "I thought I was gonna throw up before I got through the poem, but I did and then I asked her on our first date to Salinger's, and she said yes. It took a whole 'nother four months for me to ask her to be my girlfriend, but I never would've had the courage if he didn't step in like he did. Now I can do anything scared."

"Mama and me used to go to this apothecary in Clinton together every other Sunday," Korey says, crossing his arms over his chest reflectively. "The place had, like, three cats roaming around and they'd randomly shoot past your feet—I hated that. But the woman who runs the shop is really nice, and when she'd get a rare crystal or really anything new, she'd call Mama to be one of the first to come check it out. And Mama would call me to go with her every time. Just the two of us . . . I miss it."

The room's quiet again for a while, Dr. Stone trying to wait Bailey and me out, but when neither of us speaks, she holds a hand out toward Bailey. "What about you, miss?" she asks. "Any special memories you want to share?"

Bailey's eyes shoot nervously around the room and then she scoots back in the chair, hiding her face in Dante's arms.

"That's okay," Dr. Stone says sweetly, "maybe today's not the day for you." And then she turns to me. "What about you, Novah, any memories come to mind that you'd like to share?"

I inhale deeply, sitting straighter in my seat. Just about everyone else spoke, so why not? "Um, yeah. I had my first anxiety attack three years ago. I remember it was just two months after our nana Paulette passed away and she'd given me this silver necklace with a ladybug charm that I desperately loved. And then one day after a Yearbook Club meeting, I was walking home with Kedijah when I realized that it wasn't around my neck anymore. She tried to calm me down, but she couldn't, and all of a sudden I couldn't breathe right anymore, but I was only, like, a minute from our shop, so I ran. And when I turned the corner, Mama was outside cleaning the windows." I rub a finger across my lip, taking a second before I can continue. "I was a mess, and I flew into her arms crying, and I couldn't get any working words out, but it was like she immediately knew what was wrong. So she put her hands on either side of my face and blew cool air on me until she was the only thing I could focus on." Bailey peeks out from behind Dante's arm with a curious look. "And after a few minutes, I could speak again. Bai did the exact same thing for me a few weeks back," I say, smiling at her through the tears welling in my eyes. "I was freaking out—having an episode—and all I could think about was how badly I'd messed up and how desperately I needed Mama. And then, all of a sudden, it was like she was there because Bailey was with me."

Bailey peels herself from Dante's arm, giving me a coy smile behind her hands.

Dr. Stone leans over to hand me her tissue box. "That was really good, guys," she says, nodding enthusiastically. "And maybe if this becomes something you all do a bit more regularly—you know, evoking these memories and speaking them out loud randomly or intentionally—then sharing for Bailey and you all might become easier. We want remembering your parents to be something that's not *only* sad. Because the sadness, that grief—I'm sorry to say—it'll always be present, but joy should run alongside thoughts of them as well. Think about it separately and together and give it a try."

CHAPTER 21

Scripts line the table as Trinity and her coanchor Elizabeth Lou wrap up their four-hour morning show. Ari dropped me off this morning for my shadow session, making sure to stuff the lunch I'd forgotten on the back seat into my hands before speeding off to her early Saturday shift at Lively's.

When I emailed Trinity about scheduling a time to come in, I didn't expect her to sign me up for a six-hour block that included showing up an hour after she does for hair and makeup (5:30 a.m.), a quick rehearsal and revising of scripts, the morning show, lunch, and introductions to the staff. Now I wish I hadn't stayed up all night with Hailee, going on and on about how excited I was about today.

I knew news anchors were busy and hard workers, but watching Trinity in action was even more fascinating than I could've imagined. With the cue from the camera people, she phased so easily in and out of her anchor persona. She went from relaxed, talking about her weekend plans, to her commanding anchor voice with perfect posture, upbeat body language, a cheery or mournful voice depending on the story, and an uncanny ability to read the teleprompter, while simultaneously being able to throw in her own corrections and jokes without missing a beat.

I watch, amazed, trying to stay out of the way of the meteorologist, camera operators, producer, social media manager, news director, and editor in a back corner, taking detailed notes like I've never bothered to do in school before. So many people work in the background to ensure the show goes smoothly and the stories are accurate. Elizbeth and Trinity have reported a recalled sunscreen, a gas station robbery, an erratic celebrity making a promise to run in the next presidential election, a twenty-one-year-old entrepreneur with an up-and-coming hair salon, an unruly senator during a joint session of Congress in DC, a unique Thanksgiving dish, and so much more in the four-hour span, without breaking a sweat.

But when it's over, Trinity's shoulders fall and I know she's exhausted. That doesn't stop her from hopping out of her chair, saying, "Follow me!" with a wave of her hand, and introducing me to every staff member we run into on the way to the lunchroom.

"So you really get a morning call time at four thirty every day?" I ask, biting into my turkey-and-cheese brioche sandwich in her office thirty minutes later.

Trinity scoops a hearty helping of her steaming, spicy black bean soup into her mouth and grabs a napkin with a shake of her head, blowing quick breaths to cool the soup in her mouth. "Not every day," she says. "Maybe two or three days out of the week, but I still enjoy being in the field and being able to talk to people and hear their experiences."

I look at her skeptically. "Even for kids' cooking competitions or when your job sends you to recruit high schoolers for internship opportunities?"

She laughs with her head thrown back. "The cooking competitions, yes. I got to try those burgers and fries, and you'll always find me wherever free food is. Now, that recruiting event was not in my contract," she chuckles. "But it got you here, so some good came out of it."

I put my sandwich to the side, smiling at Trinity behind her glass desk full of family pictures, a computer, and a silver filing box. "It was incredible watching you work, but I mean, there has to be a downside to the job."

"Oh, the downsides are there! There's not a day that I don't go on Twitter or get an email from some self-righteous person commenting on the clothes I'm wearing, the shape of my body, the way I style my hair, or how especially grating they think my voice is. Today was a good one on the teleprompter, but when you get tongue-tied, it's always bad right before it gets awful. I saw that News Reporter Fail Compilation of me screwing up words for a minute and a half straight," she says, closing her eyes in shame. "And then there's the early call times, which I have a love-hate relationship with, leaning more toward hate.

"But, at the end of the day, I can't pretend that I don't love this job. I love the opportunities for me to learn and grow and earn more responsibility around here. I love prepping for shows, and I love that I've been put in this position to share what's going on in the world with those who may otherwise be clueless. Novah, people really trust us. They trust us to feed them truth, and I don't take that for granted. I approach every story with kindness and empathy, because I realize that these stories we're sharing have real-life people behind them who deserve respect. This job," she says, gesturing around the room, "my career. It means the world to me."

I shake my head, and Trinity looks confused. "Not what you wanted to hear?"

"Nope. Not at all. I was honestly hoping something I'd hear or see today would turn me off from wanting to get this internship, but you're right. I love it here too. I love the environment, I love how everyone's working together and how you and Elizabeth feed off each other. You guys, like, know the exact amount of energy each story needs, y'all knew how to improvise and still stay on track, and I've only ever imagined how difficult reading off a teleprompter is, but you made it look easy."

Trinity pretends to brush dirt off her shoulder, having wrapped her blue blazer behind her chair, and leans in. "Well, Novah, I'm thrilled you enjoyed yourself—one of the kids who signed up to shadow Elizabeth fell asleep in a corner two hours in a week ago, but why would you hope something would turn you away from the internship? You seemed so enthused on your application."

I grimace, and my eyes fall to Mama's bracelet. "Can I be honest?"

"Of course."

"My sister knew I secretly really wanted this and filled out the application and wrote that essay in my name. That's why it came from her email."

"Ah," Trinity says, placing her spoon on her napkin. "Okay, that makes a lot more sense. But why was *wanting* this internship a secret?"

I shrug. "If I could convince myself that I didn't want it, then it would hurt less to have to turn it down. In the case that I'm actually offered it," I add quickly.

"And why on earth would you turn this position down if you want it?"

I bite my lip, unsure of how much of our real

chaotic home life is okay to reveal. From the outside looking in, it might look like we're running our home semi-smoothly. Or at least it might've looked that way for the last two weeks. But very few people know about the fights, the accidental fire, the missing homework assignments, forgotten bills, broken appliances, or our struggles to keep it together. Just recently, we've begun to really figure things out, and that's mostly because of outside help. Not because we know what we're doing. Not because we have a true handle on how we're supposed to go on without Mama and Daddy. How could I dedicate my time here when we're just getting on track?

"It's just . . . between my family, school, and working at the shop, I don't think I'd have the time. Life is always hectic, and I pretend that I'm holding everything together really well, but I mess up a lot. You can't even imagine," I say, and slowly exhale. "My sister Ari . . . well, I haven't exactly made things easy on her, but I want to now! When she looks at me, I want her to be able to know that she can trust me. If I started giving part of myself and my time to an internship, I don't think I'd be able to keep up. And if I'm being really honest . . . I don't know if I deserve all of this either."

Trinity stares at me for a while with a squint and then turns toward her desktop and scrolls for a minute. "*Hello, Ms. Dawson,*" she reads. "*This is my sister*

Novah Wilkinson's application. I may be overstepping, but picking Novah would be the best decision for this program and a dream come true for her even if she tries playing the nonchalant card. I hear that you were familiar with our parents, and losing them was the most painful thing any of us has ever experienced and will ever experience. But Novah was the first of us to bounce back and force us up with her. She goes out of her way to help everyone she comes in contact with; she's a hard worker, compassionate where others fall short, attentive, and deserving of a chance to figure out who she wants to be outside of her roles as a sister and a caretaker. If Novah's awarded the opportunity to work as an intern at Channel 4 News, she will not disappoint. Ariana Wilkinson."

I feel a prickle in the back of my eyes. I rub them, muttering about allergy season and forcing myself to breathe deeply as Trinity waits. "Ari really said all that?" is all I'm able to manage. It's embarrassing how my voice shakes, but Trinity just scoffs, turning the screen to face me. Ari sent that the same day as Korey's cooking competition.

"I can forward you the email if you'd like? Novah, your sister and your friend have this consistent faith in you—faith that you seem to be missing yourself. That much is clear. Ariana knows you can do it and based on this, I'm willing to bet she'd help you figure out your home situation if earning this internship becomes your reality." Trinity turns the screen back, leaning forward on folded hands. "You're the only one counting yourself out. Do you really want to do that?"

I lean back in my chair with a huff. Ari still thinks I deserve this after everything I've done. She literally woke me up in time and drove me here this morning. Even after the way I treated her and disregarded her, she still thinks I can do it.

"You made a childish, teenage, stupid mistake, but I can accept your apology because whether it feels like it or not, you are still a kid. And kids mess up. Hell, you see me screw up every day! But I know we'll eventually get better at this life thing. We have to." That's what she said to me when I asked her "how" days after my accident. And she's right. Why do I keep trying to convince myself I don't deserve to pursue a dream when everyone around me is pushing me toward it?

I sit up, shaking my head fervently. "Won't happen again."

Trinity's face splits into a smile, and then her computer pings with a new email. "Looks like the set's free for at least an hour," she says, popping out of her chair. "C'mon. I'll let you sit at the desk for a few quick pics, and you can even try reading off the teleprompter if you wanna."

CHAPTER 22

Zion hands the wet plate to me, and I dry it with the dishcloth before handing it to Bailey. She sits on the counter, placing it carefully in our overflowing dish rack. We already have a load going in the dishwasher after a hearty Thanksgiving meal and half a sink of dishes to go.

Korey and Dante are at the dining room table, putting leftovers into Tupperware. We'll be eating turkey, mac 'n' cheese, collards, and sweet potatoes for at least the next week and a half.

"Thanksgiving was Daddy's favorite holiday," I say, more to myself than to Zion. I'd been thinking it all day and just wanted the words to be out there. He liked to try new recipes every year, but they weren't always a success.

"Remember those cheesy scalloped potatoes he made last year instead of mac 'n' cheese?" Zion asks, taking the thought out of my head.

"Ugh, oh right! He put, like, five different cheeses in it and there was a layer of oil, like, sitting on top of it."

217

"I liked it," Bailey signs.

"It was gross," Korey says, walking into the kitchen, his hands overflowing with full containers. He nudges the fridge door open with his knee. "My mac 'n' cheese was better."

This was Korey's first year making the turkey, with a little assistance from Zion. I tried to offer to help early this morning, but he shooed me out of the kitchen before I could finish asking. Besides the Hawaiian rolls that Ari popped in the oven, he'd basically prepared the entire meal.

Dante sulks in with the last of the Tupperware, hands them to Korey, and plops into a chair at the table. Unlike the rest of us, he's been a bit more visibly sad about missing Mama and Daddy for our first major holiday without them.

I dry the cutlery in my hands, sharing an uneasy look with Zion.

Zion turns, leaning on the sink with crossed arms. "My favorite part about today was watching the Macy's Thanksgiving Day Parade after Korey kicked me out of the kitchen."

"Mine was the sweet potatoes with those perfectly browned marshmallows," I say, picking up his lead.

Bailey taps a finger to her chin, and then her hands fly. "My favorite part was playing Uno with you and Ari. I won three times! And I'm the best at Twister."

"Mine's gonna be the nap I take after we're done straightening up," Korey says.

I throw the damp rag on my shoulder, bending in front of Dante. "What about you? What was your favorite part?"

He picks his head up, gathering his lips from one side to the other. "I had a dream before I woke up that we were all with Mama and Daddy again. I liked that."

I bite the inside of my mouth, not knowing what to say to make him feel better. And then my eyes find the fresh bouquet of pink and lavender roses on the counter. They arrived this morning. The card read "*I know that it'll be a tough one, but you guys can get through anything together. Love, Antoinette and Omari.*"

We can get through this together, we just need to be near Mama and Daddy.

"Well, why don't we go visit their headstones," I say, beckoning to him.

Dante looks unsure at first, almost frightened. And then his face splits into a smile. "I think that would make me feel better."

"What would make you feel better?" Ari asks from behind me. I hadn't heard her. She stands at the foot of the steps with Miles on her hip, now glistening from the lotion after his bath. When he stood from the table after eating, collard greens slid down the leg of his pants and hit the floor. Zion, Korey, and I yelled "not it" before Ari, so she was stuck with bath time.

I should've brought it up with her first before I said anything to Dante, but I just couldn't help it with the look on his face.

"I was just thinking—"

"Novah thinks it would be cool if we visited the grave site today," Zion says, stepping up beside me. "I think it's a good idea." He shrugs.

"Me too," Korey says.

I stand with my heartbeat quickening. Maybe it's too soon for her? And am I even ready? I'd offered, but I imagine standing in front of their graves will feel different than just thinking about it.

Surprisingly Ari's face doesn't give anything away. She's been a bit off today too. I caught her going out of her way to avoid looking at the altar more than once, and when Antoinette's flowers were delivered this morning, she read the card, gave a sad smile, and silently left the room. Five minutes later, she came back with puffy eyes, but a real smile, when she held out the Uno cards to Bailey.

She places Miles in a chair, scratching anxiously at the back of her neck, and bends in front of Dante where I just was.

"You really think that would help you today, bud?"

He nods fervently.

"All right." She claps. "Sweaters on; it'll probably get chilly."

◇◇◇

Thirty minutes later, we cruise up the street packed in the SUV, bobbing our heads to "Never Too Much" on 96.3. It's fitting, almost kismet. This was the song Mama and Daddy first danced to at their small wedding before any of us were thought of. I grab Bailey's trembling hand beside me, pointing toward horses galloping as we pass a small farm. As we make a left on Woodyard Road, we see the brick wall and tall black gates of Resurrection Cemetery—our parents' final resting place. But my heart drops to my stomach. The gates are closed.

Ari slows down but continues to drive until we're just an inch from them. Maybe she thought the gates were motion sensored from the street, but the padlock is clear as day from here.

Her hands drop from the wheel as we all sit stewing in disappointment. It took us almost seven months to make it here, and now—nothing?

"I'm sorry, guys," I exhale when no one else says a

word. "I didn't think to check the website to see their operating hours."

"And it's a major holiday," Zion says. "We should've guessed."

The roses Dante holds drop in his lap, and then I hear his first sniffle.

Miles leans forward in his car seat. "We can't see Mama and Daddy, Ari?"

She turns to him, her face a bundle of emotions until she unclicks her seat belt, throws open the door, and hops out. We sit there, watching her jog in her Uggs up the short grassy hill where the black words *Resurrection Cemetery* lie on the lower brick wall. She walks up to it, stands back with her arms crossed, and tilts her head to the side.

Zion realizes that she's sizing up the wall at the same time as I do, turning in the passenger seat to beam at me.

"Let's give it a try," Ari calls. And then we're all unbuckling our seat belts, slamming the car doors shut and running to meet her on the hill.

"It's not too bad of a climb," she says, looking at me. "What do you think?"

The wall only has a few inches on Zion's six-foot frame.

"Let's do it." I nod.

Ari goes over first with a boost from Zion. And one

by one—Miles second, followed by Bailey, Dante, Korey, and me, we climb over the wall. I lean over, with the brick bearing into my stomach as Ari and Korey hold my feet, and reach for Zion. He only needs a slight pull before he gathers his footing and launches himself over too.

After an eight-minute walk, we find the headstones. Resurrection Cemetery is something of a Wilkinson resting place, so we've all been here before with Mama and Daddy to visit Nana Paulette, Paum, Cousin Jerome, and Aunt Monnie. But we've never been here without them. Technically, we still haven't.

A picture of Mama and Daddy on their wedding day smiles up at us on the dark gray headstone with the inscription *Dearly loved and never forgotten* under their names and birth and ascension dates. The scripture Isaiah 41:13 lies beneath the inscription.

Dante moves toward the headstone, while the rest of us stand maybe six feet away. I can hear Ari's soft cries beside me and see Zion wrap an arm around her shoulder as he takes the pink and lavender roses out of the plastic bag. Korey moves beside him with scissors and clips the long ends of the stems. With Miles's help, Dante places the roses in the flower holder, but they don't step back to where we are. Korey bends in front of their headstone like he does in front of the altar, muttering soft words I can't make out with his eyes shut. He's quiet for a moment but stays put. And then Miles drops to his knees too, looking up at Korey. And Dante does the same. Soon Ari, Zion, Bailey, and I are on bended knee too, forming a half crescent around the headstone.

"Does anyone want to say anything?" Ari asks after a minute or so.

"It's been really hard here without you guys," Dante starts with tears streaming down his face. "But I'm happy now that we're all back together." He takes a deep shuddering breath and Korey takes his hand. "I hope we can come back soon to be with you guys again."

"We will, D," Zion promises.

And then Bailey raises her hand as if we're still in Dr. Stone's office. I hear things in the small unicorn bag she wears shift when her arm shoots in the air. Ari gives her head a slight nod. "Are Mama and Daddy here?" she signs.

"This is where we buried their bodies," I say, smiling at her, "but really they're wherever we are."

"I have a memory now. Will they hear me?"

"Of course they'll hear you, Bai," Korey says, nudging her on.

But Bailey pulls her arm out of the strap on her backpack and unzips the bag full of snacks, her doll, and the small dry-erase board she's carried around for months. She takes out the board, leaning forward to place it beside the headstone.

When she clears her throat, my eyes tear away from my parents' picture and land on her. All our eyes are on Bailey, waiting. And then she speaks.

"M-me and Mama grew pretty flowers," she starts slowly. Her voice comes out a bit raspy, but she looks confidently at their picture. I feel Ari grip my wrist—holding on to me like an anchor—but none of us dares interrupt her. "Last time, we got marigold seeds in a yellow bag. Mama said we had to wait weeks for them to grow. And then they did." She smiles brightly at them. "Daddy told me they grew tall and beautiful like me." Bailey looks up at Zion. "When it's hot again, can we grow flowers?"

He nods at her with wide eyes. "We can grow anything you like, Bai."

I bite my lip, wiping at my eyes with my sweatshirt sleeve.

"Even watermelon?" Miles asks excitedly.

I laugh, looking at his big eyes. "We can try."

"That's such a good idea for us to grow flowers and watermelon to honor them," Ari says. Her nose is stuffy, but she's cheesing too.

"And when they grow, we can bring them back here as an offering?" Korey suggests.

Dante nods eagerly, saying, "I wish we could do

something else to honor them too. Something even bigger."

"Bigger than watermelon?" Miles asks, confused.

"Yes, bigger than watermelon," I say, poking his stomach.

"We do have to do something bigger, guys," Ari says with a hesitant half smile. Goose bumps spread across my skin, and I know what's coming is gonna hurt, so I clench my fist, digging my nails into my palm. "I didn't want to say anything," she continues, "because it's Thanksgiving, but it's better if we're all aware of what's coming. I got the call from Ms. Lusby late last night, and with everything that's gone on recently, our custody hearing date was pushed up." She bites her top lip, taking a moment to look at each of us with reassurance even as I hear her breaths getting shallow. "Ms. Lusby will be there, maybe even Dr. Stone. And I know things have been . . . shaky recently, but I still think we have a real chance at this. We're gonna honor Mama and Daddy in two weeks by making sure that we stay together. The plan is to go in with confidence, because even if the judge needs a bit of convincing, we all know that the best place for each of us is with each other. It's what they would want."

I look from Ari to Zion and Korey and pull at the concentration and determination in each of their eyes until I feel a bit of it myself.

"We can do this," I say, nodding at Dante, Bailey, and Miles, willing the words to sound way more confident than I feel.

Ari grins. "It's getting cold," she says, standing, and we all follow her lead. "Let's get home!"

CHAPTER 23

I knock on the open white door before peeking in and seeing Dr. Stone's face break into a smile.

"Novah," she says, closing the book she's holding. "Come on in and take a seat."

I do as she says, removing my puffy jacket and laying it on the couch beside my book bag. Dr. Stone sits in front of me with her long, curly hair wrapped partially in a neat headscarf and a curious look in her eyes.

I scratch nervously at my neck, saying, "I'm really sorry to drop in on you without notice, but I was just hoping it would be okay for me to talk to you for a few minutes."

"Of course it's fine. I'm happy you stopped by. Especially since I couldn't get a single word out of you yesterday. What's up?"

That's the thing. I don't really know why I'm here. Zion is picking the kids up from school so I could stay for the Student Grief Support Group. And I thought I might really give it a try today, but when I looked through the window of the meeting room, there was already a guy in full-blown tears being consoled by Summer. Walking through that door would have been dreadful. But Dr. Stone's been on my mind all day. Really since I left our family therapy session last night. That in itself was a full-blown sob session brought on when Ari admitted to a recurring dream she's been having about coming home to an empty house after the custody hearing. Bailey panicked when she came to the realization that we don't know how long our separation could last. And Ari had to explain to poor Miles that separating doesn't mean we leave like Mama and Daddy did. Then Zion asked about appeal processes, Korey flat out said he'd run away, and Dante asked what he should do if a foster parent hits him.

But I just sat there listening to their fears, stone-faced and unable to really comprehend how we ended up here.

I give Dr. Stone a sad shrug. "I guess I'm just really uneasy because of the hearing tomorrow. I haven't been able to sleep, and really it all boils down to the fact that . . . I'm scared," I whisper. When I say the words out loud, I feel some of the tension in my neck release. I know that fear has been the primary emotion in our home since our parents died, but I don't know if I've ever said the words out loud. I blow out a calming rush of air.

Dr. Stone nods knowingly. "And that felt good to

say, even though all that same fear is still there, right?"

"Yeah, it does," I say quietly.

"Makes sense. That's a big reason why I wanted you all to do the worst-case scenario exercise yesterday. Because of the release so many of us feel when we can admit what the root of our problems is even if doing so isn't an automatic fix. Every single day of your life, you are constantly with yourself and there's no escape from that. But being self-aware doesn't have to mean your own brain is holding you hostage. You don't have to be shackled to every bad feeling you have, and admitting those feelings to the people who understand best what you're going through, Novah, can be the release you need."

She reaches toward the box of tissues sitting on her glass side table and hands them to me when a single tear streams down my cheek.

"Now, I do remember Ariana telling me that you were going to attend your school's grief support group today, but since you're here, I'm guessing that didn't work out. And that's okay," she says, nodding. "But I also recall you telling me that you didn't want to go because sitting with your classmates discussing why you're sad won't help. But maybe sitting with your siblings and sharing your fear will feel different. You don't know how things will go tomorrow, so tell them with your words what they need to hear today."

Seven months ago, I was fighting to free myself from my family. I'd forgotten what it meant to be limitless even while I was surrounded by love. But when Mama and Daddy died, I was certain that not only were my dreams dead, love was too. I rediscovered love quickly when Ariana wrapped her arms around me that same night. Now freedom for me only exists in a world where my siblings and I are together. My dreams feel attainable with them because they're constantly pushing me to be better. I can be my truest self and know I'm wanted—know I'm loved regardless with them. And I feel like I can breathe with them.

What happens tomorrow if the judge takes my breath away?

◊◊◊

We all sit in the living room lit only by the white candles Korey has placed on every solid surface. Incense burns, soft instrumentals play from Zion's laptop, and there's a reflective calm that's settled over us despite the knowledge that this very well may be our last night together for a long while.

I look around the room, watching Ari, Dante, and Korey putting together a puzzle; Miles and Bailey drawing in her sketch pad; Zion reading; Powder sleeping in my lap as I stroke his thick fur. And the portrait of Mama and Daddy my friends and Hailee gifted us this afternoon hanging on the wall before us all. The card said *You're all prepped for the worst, so it's time to hope for the best.*

I almost don't want to say a word to disrupt our peace, but I know Dr. Stone was right earlier. I don't want to miss this opportunity to be completely truthful, especially when I don't know when I'll get another chance.

I clear my throat, and every pair of eyes turns toward me as I start slowly saying, "I went to Dr. Stone's office today after school because I was trying to sort out some of my emotions. And I think she helped me see things more clearly than I have in a while."

"Well, I thought you were going to SGSG," Ari says, propping herself up on her elbows, "but ... I guess it's even better you talked to Dr. Stone."

Miles nods fervently, saying, "She's nice!"

"And smart," Bailey whispers.

Zion places his book on the coffee table. "What did she help you see?"

I twist the brown crystals on my wrist, but keep my eyes on my siblings. "She helped me see that I should've taken the opportunity yesterday to share that I'm just as scared as all of you about how tomorrow will end. I'm scared of the unknown and the possibilities of what could happen if we're not there to protect one another.

And I'm scared of being alone and having to try to start all over again to find another new normal."

"Me too," Dante says quietly. When Korey automatically wraps an arm around him, pulling him closer, I smile.

"But I also think that regardless of what happens tomorrow, I'm positive Mama and Daddy would be proud of us for continuing to live our lives fully and for how we've each taken care of each other. Daddy always said that parenting was about preparing your children to succeed even after they're gone. And I know he didn't plan for them to transition when they did. But when I look at us now and how we've loved one another, I know they did their job well.

"We belong with one another, and I'll never stop fighting to make sure everyone knows it."

CHAPTER 24

As we dressed in business casual this morning, the eerie silence was reminiscent of the one I felt on the morning of Mama and Daddy's funeral. But seeing Hailee, Kedijah, and Antoinette in front of the courthouse when we pulled up lifted just a bit of the suffocating pressure. Even seeing Ms. Lusby and Dr. Stone inside the hearing room gave a small sense of relief. It was a reminder that this day didn't have to end in doom.

Judge Odell is a very to-the-business type of man, and our hearing starts with Ms. Lusby giving a review of her relevant notes, observations over her last six visits, and a closing statement that surprises me, considering how stern she's been since she confronted us at Lively's last month.

"While Ariana is clearly young and just getting the hang of parenting her siblings while simultaneously inheriting their parents' dog-grooming business, she's approaching both tasks with a determined commitment to succeed, evidenced by her readiness to put her family first. Not only do I believe she can do this, but I've spoken to each of her siblings thoroughly and have witnessed myself the full confidence they have in her and each other."

Now Ariana is called and stands, but not before turning and flashing an almost-panicked expression at Zion and me. I recognize the look. Her bunched brows, pinched lips, and wild eyes. While other athletes often walk onto the court with their game faces on, Ari always used to look like this before her volleyball games—scared out of her mind—only to go out and dominate every single time.

"Ms. Wilkinson," Judge Odell says, glancing up at her from something on his desk. "What can you tell me of the progress of the children under your care?"

She clears her throat. "Only that they're each remaining on track and surpassing the expectations of our parents even after our loss." She raises a finger, pointing at each of us while she speaks. "Miles, who's five, is meeting all of his milestones, social with every person and pet he meets, and is advanced in reading comprehension. That should all be in the file sent directly from his teacher. Bailey, aged seven, is reading at a fourth-grade level, a gifted artist, compassionate, and an empath. I'm not sure if you'd like to see, but I have pictures of her drawings—she's very talented. Dante, ten years old, is an aspiring paleontologist or astronaut who skipped a grade last year and is maintaining a 4.0 GPA with ease in the sixth grade. Korey, thirteen, is the chef of the family and won the City Teen Burger Competition in October that came with a cash prize in addition to a full scholarship to the prestigious Rochester Culinary Camp in New York this summer—we're very proud of him. Novah has the skill set to run our shop, Lively Pups, on her own at just sixteen. She's organized, a problem solver, has a strong work ethic, and is trustworthy. In addition to all of that, she is a finalist in the running to earn an internship at Channel Four News under news anchor and journalist Trinity Dawson. And Zion, who will be eighteen in February, received his first acceptance email from the University of Maryland this morning with a scholarship—that can be forwarded to you as well. We're hoping to celebrate tonight if things go accordingly."

Now Dr. Stone takes the stage, and the questions are more about our emotional readiness, maturity, and nurturing. Especially considering Judge Odell's previous concerns about Bailey's failure to verbally communicate.

"I've received the notes from Bailey Wilkinson's speech therapist, and we are in agreement that she never truly stopped speaking to anyone who speaks American Sign Language. As you are aware, each of the seven Wilkinsons, including five-year-old Miles, is fluent in ASL and has been since Bailey was three years old. Ariana and her siblings have followed through in increasing Bailey's speech therapy sessions, and she hasn't missed one since Ariana was granted conditional custody. So that she could communicate with those not proficient in ASL, the siblings have provided Bailey with a dry-erase board. And I recently understand that within the last couple of weeks, Bailey has slowly begun speaking verbally to all her siblings in the house."

Judge Odell looks at Ari beside me from his stand, simply asking, "Is that true, Ms. Wilkinson?"

"Yes, Your Honor, it is," Ariana says quickly. "She first spoke to us when we visited our parents' grave on Thanksgiving Day."

Bailey nods vehemently from Zion's lap.

The only sign of emotion crossing Judge Odell's face is a quick raise of his brows, and I can't tell if the look is intrigue or disbelief before he begins questioning Dr. Stone about Korey's schooling progress.

Half an hour later, when Dr. Stone is asked to take her seat, Judge Odell slides a pair of old wire glasses onto his face just to peer over them as he looks through a stack of papers. It's three minutes of nervous glances between us, reassuring and calm looks from Ms. Lusby and Dr. Stone, and encouraging smiles from Hailee, Kedijah, and Antoinette behind us.

My head hurts from the constant pounding that'd set in since we sat on these cold, hard wooden chairs, and my right leg is cramping from the involuntary nervous bounce I can't still.

My phone buzzes in my pocket and I pull it out discreetly.

> **Trinity:** *Just got word from my supervisor and wanted to be the first to let you know. You were picked for the internship starting mid-January!!!!!! It's a commitment, and I know you were worried about scheduling, but it'll be flexible and I'm willing to work with you!*

My heart swells, and I feel like I could skip before I look up and remember where I am. A second later, my phone buzzes again with the official acceptance email, but when I see Judge Odell remove his glasses, I stuff my phone in my purse.

Clasping his hands in front of us, he says, "While the statements I've received today from Ariana Wilkinson, Dr. Johnetta Stone, and Ms. June Lusby have all been extremely compelling, I do need time for further deliberation in my chambers."

My mouth goes dry and I feel sweat forming on the back of my neck at his words. I want this to be over and I want him to come to the right decision now.

What more is there for him to consider? How much longer is he going to hold our futures in his hands?

"But," he says just as my foot tapping sets into overdrive, "I'd like to open the floor up to any of the Wilkinson children right now. Would any of you like to give a statement before I leave for deliberation?"

My hand shoots into the air before I can properly comprehend what I've just done. But even as I glance up at my arm in the air and the tiger's-eye crystal hanging from my wrist, I don't pull it down.

"Novah, aged sixteen. Is that right?" Judge Odell asks, deadpan.

I nod quickly, feeling my heartbeat even in the tips of each of my fingers.

"What would you like to say?"

I push myself up from my seat, looking from my right at Zion, Bailey, Korey, Miles, and Dante gazing up expectantly, to my left, where Ari gives a fervent nod. I slide my moist hands down the rough fabric of my slacks and take a deep breath.

"Your Honor, as you can probably imagine, losing our parents, Ezekiel and Lisa, back in May was the most painful thing any of us could have ever experienced. We're still experiencing that pain, as a matter of fact. And honestly, with all of the chaos and confusion that comes with being in a family of seven, while keeping a business running, it sometimes feels like our lives are just picking up the pieces of one unfortunate situation after another. But more often what we experience are the highs that come from being with each other every single day. Sometimes the wins are smaller, like Miles learning to tie his shoes last week or Bailey winning her spelling bee or even Dante bringing home another A-plus on an assignment that the rest of us probably would've struggled with. Other times the wins feel bigger, like Korey winning the cooking competition, Zion getting into college, or even the letter of acceptance I just received for the news anchor internship—I can forward that to you, by the way." I rub my hands together anxiously as Judge Odell just stares down at me, his blank face unchanging. "My point is, is that I think it's so important that we get to continue to experience the good and the bad, and every single win together. And we can only do that if you make that decision today, Your Honor. I understand that handing this much responsibility to an eighteen-year-old may seem like a lot or even unfair from some points of view. But my sister has never hesitated to live up to the challenge, no matter what's been thrown at her. Ariana was supposed to be at Howard this fall on a volleyball scholarship and had to give that up to raise us. But she hasn't given up on her dreams despite that. She's in school, taking classes at the community college, and even aced her midterms too—I don't know if you already knew that. She did that while also pushing each of us to pursue our own goals and encouraging us to never stop dreaming despite our own doubts and even working behind the scenes to make this internship dream happen for me when I felt like it was impossible. She's been everything we've needed her to be and more, and I'll be grateful to her for the rest of my life." I bite down hard on my bottom lip, hoping I'm helping and not hurting our case. "My parents were love. They worked hard and they made sure to instill those same values in us. And I just hope that you continue to allow us to do life together."

◊◊◊

The seven of us sit huddled together in the front of the courtroom, having the same conversation over and over.

"Are you guys sure I didn't say too much?" I ask, biting my nails, on the verge of tears. At the moment, it felt like the right thing to do, and I couldn't just not say nothing. But it feels like Judge Odell has been in his chamber for far too long. What else did he need to look over? Was describing our family as chaotic a mistake? Was it taking so long so they could make sure the people who would be separating us have enough time to get here? "Maybe I should've just shut up."

"Nov, no, it was good," Zion whispers. "You gave him another perspective."

Korey nods. "I liked it. Pulled on the old heartstrings and all that."

"And it was all true," Dante says shakily. He looks just as scared as me. "He had to believe you!"

Bailey takes his hand in hers, stroking his palm with her thumb.

"I can say some things too. And I know he'll listen because I'll tell him to," Miles says, bouncing on the balls of his feet.

"I think it's a little too late for you to say anything now, bud." Ari reaches for Miles, pulling him to her lap. And beckoning us all to look at her. "Everybody just calm down a bit, okay. Dr. Stone knew exactly what she was doing, Ms. Lusby was actually trying really hard to help us, and Novah," she says, turning to face me, "every single word you said today was gold. We have to believe it was enough."

We startle when the bailiff announces Judge Odell, and I feel like I'm going to be sick when he reenters the courtroom. The room is still and seems to be collectively holding its breath as he takes his seat, straightens himself in his chair, and looks down on us all.

"I'm not one to waste time, so I won't continue

to have you all wait for my decision," Judge Odell says seriously. "After careful deliberation, and review of every document, note, or observation I have received on this family, I rule that as of today, Ariana Wilkinson will receive full custody without condition of the six Wilkinson children, her siblings Miles, Bailey, Dante, Korey, Novah, and Zion." And then the old man smiles at Ariana as her mouth hangs open, her face frozen in a gasp. "Ms. Wilkinson, I have confidence that you will take on this responsibility with the utmost care and highest level of regard. Congratulations." And with a bang of his gavel, he's gone.

Ariana waits until the door shuts behind Judge Odell before she lets out her first squeal of glee, and then we're all following her lead. My insides rocket as she pins my arms to my sides in a bear hug, and when she lets go, Bailey bounds to me. I hold her in my arms and Zion consoles Dante and his happy sobs as Miles hugs Korey around the knees.

Tears stream down my face. Happy tears. I don't know that I've ever cried happy tears before, but it feels like a dream when Antoinette, Hailee, and Kedijah come join in the celebration too.

We argue, we make mistakes. We're chaotic and almost fell apart a dozen times since our parents ascended, but we're being allowed to stay together.

Together in business, together in life, and together in love. That's what they taught us. For the first time since last May, I smile with confidence, knowing that we can do this. We can make it, succeed, and thrive even in our "after."

ACKNOWLEDGMENTS

Authors always say the second book is notoriously hard to write, and I can now confirm that to be 1,000 percent true. But I'm SO pleased with the result of the heart I poured into Novah and the Wilkinson siblings' story.

I'd like to first shout a special thanks to my Lord and Savior, Jesus Christ, for guiding, redirecting, and loving me every step of the way.

To Carmell, Antoine, and Alyssa: I'm only able to communicate what true siblinghood looks like in my books because of our real-life experiences growing up. We get on each other's nerves in ridiculous ways, but there's *nothing* I wouldn't do for you all.

To my parents, James and Felicia: I owe you everything for tolerating my endless whining alone, but you've done so much more. I've watched you bend over backward and parent far more than your own children, and I love you for it. But I also just love both of you for being yourselves. I don't know how I'd find my way in your absence.

Jas, thank you for responding to all my over-whelmed texts, calls, and emails with calmness and ease. I count you as a friend and the best agent I could've dreamed of. Mallory, your advice that "we're writing books, not performing brain surgery" actually allowed me to sleep at night. Thank you for your invaluable guidance and feedback.

Thank you to everyone at Scholastic who has worked behind the scenes for *As Long as We're Together*, especially Cassy Price; Janell Harris; Mariclaire Jastremsky; the sales, marketing, and publicity teams; and the Scholastic Book Clubs and Book Fairs. Camellia Jiles, you illustrated this cover and communicated the love and care I wrote into this book so flawlessly. Thank you, a million times over!

Krista, we've spent more late nights than I can count talking about our woes, our writing dreams, and our futures. Thank you for being my quarantine partner, roommate, and friend.

To my fellow authors, the publishing community, and my readers: Living this dream as a writer would literally be impossible without you. Thank you for paving the way and believing in me. I promise to pull those behind me up every step of the way.

So many things that I love went into this book: the undying devotion and appreciation I have for my family, my obsession with television and cinema, my adoration for children, and my understanding of the roles our loved ones and ancestors play when we're suddenly left here without them. I tried my very best to handle the topics of survival after loss and ongoing grief in a sensitive manner, and I hope that is communicated clearly on the page.

ABOUT THE AUTHOR

Brianna Peppins is the author of young adult contemporary books, including *Briarcliff Prep* and *As Long as We're Together*. She was raised in Prince George's County, Maryland, and graduated from Spelman College with a BA in psychology. When not writing, Brianna takes special interest in spending time with her loved ones and social justice issues, and is a self-proclaimed movie aficionado. Visit her online at briannapeppins.com, on Twitter at @Lexi_pep, and on Instagram at @Lexi_pep.